INSPIRE

WILLIAM SWANN

9 8 7 6 5 4 3 2 1

First Edition
PRINTED IN THE UNITED STATES OF AMERICA
Heritage Publishing
Cover Design: CTS Graphics

978-0-9987766-8-2

Acknowledgments

I want to express my deepest gratitude to my wife, Connie, for her unwavering support and encouragement throughout this writing journey. Her belief in my abilities and her motivation have been instrumental in bringing this book to fruition. Without her love and understanding, this project would not have been possible.

I want to thank my mother-in-law, Ella B. Young, for her loving and faithful support of me and my family over many years. She's been a wise and trusted member of our family, and we wouldn't be where we are today without her.

My children—Sebastian; London; LA; and Danyeal—and my grandson, Andrew have always been my pillars of strength. They have inspired me to experience a passion for leadership and personal growth so that I can be an example to future generations, and I am grateful for their faith in me. I also appreciate my sister Jerry for the life lessons she taught me while she was in my care. As a whole, my family has taught me the ropes of leadership and inspired me to climb.

Incredible people have influenced my career, and I have been privileged to work with many of them. I would like to acknowledge their impact on my life. Their diverse perspectives, collaborative spirit, and shared experiences have shaped my understanding of leadership and greatly influenced the content of this book. I am indebted to each of them for their contributions and for the lessons I have learned from our collective journey.

My life experiences have shaped me into who I am today, and I am thankful for all of them. Every challenge, triumph, and moment of self-reflection has played a significant role in helping me to navigate different stages of leadership. Through these experiences, I have gained the insights and wisdom I hope to impart through this book.

Most importantly, I thank God for His boundless love and infinite blessings. I am humbled by His presence and forever grateful for the opportunities He has provided me. I want to continue seeking His guidance and striving to use the wisdom and knowledge He has bestowed on me for the greater good.

Contents

Introduction

At this point, I've risen through the ranks and met many of my life's goals. I've gone from firefighter to engineer to training officer to captain, and today I'm the fire chief of the Nashville Fire Department. In taking on this position, I also experienced many firsts in the department: I'm the first paramedic, the youngest person, and the first African American to become chief. So my leadership journey has been filled with many professional and personal achievements that have made me and my family proud.

But I'm not satisfied with climbing the career ladder and accumulating accomplishments and accolades only for myself. I also want to be a leader of leaders and inspire them to discover their potential. I wrote this book to help current and future leaders develop and strengthen the key qualities and characteristics I've acquired on my leadership journey.

Great leaders are confident and responsible. They have an indelible vision for their organization and communicate that vision efficiently and effectively. They invite those they lead to unify around their vision and create a committed and vibrant community that sets and achieves goals that further the mission of the organization. That sums up the knowledge that most people have about leaders.

However, I'd like to encourage leaders to reach their highest potential. My personal and professional life is grounded in my relationship with Jesus Christ. As a Christian, I strive to work in a spirit of excellence that bears witness to my strong faith. So I want to inspire leaders also to consider becoming servant leaders who are open to learning; who will lead with integrity, courage, and compassion; and who will fuel their leadership with passion.

Great leaders develop and strengthen the most important qualities that enable them to be effective and productive. The life of a leader is not an easy one, but I have found that it can be extremely rewarding. Leaders may reap many awards and accomplishments, but they can also touch the lives of many people in positive and lasting ways.

Chapter One

Commitment

What do you do when it seems your sacrifices aren't worth it? How do you persevere through adversity and setbacks? Balancing sacrifice and commitment is often difficult, but we know that our level of commitment is essential to our effectiveness and success. Through the ups and downs of my career, I've often asked myself, *What am I doing? Have I made the right decisions? Is the present struggle worth it? Can I hold firm to my convictions for the long term? Am I dedicated enough to my vision for the future?*

Several years ago, I was at a great point in my career. I was a captain in the fire department with a decent track record of accomplishments. At this point, I had come through the ranks from firefighter to engineer to captain to training officer. I assisted with public relations for the department and was part of a four-person team that revived our color and honor guard. I was always respectful of the department's vision while trying to do whatever was asked of me. I wanted to advance in the department, so I was making plans for what was next.

Many of us have heard the expression "If you want to make God laugh, tell Him your plans." I'm not comparing

God to the chief of the fire department, but I want to illustrate how God can use people to disrupt our best-laid plans and bring us into places in ways we never imagined. I will share with you a story that will take many pieces of a delicate puzzle to come together to display a successful ongoing picture. It would not happen overnight or by chance, and I don't believe in luck. Where I am today involves timing, the support of the right people, hard work, and a lot of sacrifices. More importantly, it involves God's blessings.

I received a call from the director chief, who occupied the highest position in the fire department. He was once my instructor when I was a recruit at the academy, and he became my mentor. He was intelligent, robust, sincere, and driven. One day, he called me to his office and told me about his vision for our department while also sharing his succession plan. He told me who he wanted to take his place when he retired. He believed that I had what it took to become the next director chief of the department.

The Nashville Fire Department was established in 1860, and he was the eighteenth director. If I became his successor, many pieces would have to fall in place because becoming director chief is a huge task as well as a major accomplishment. But although he wanted me to be his successor, there were no guarantees this would happen. However, his job was to prepare me the best he could and give me a bird's eye view of how things worked.

If I became the next director chief, I would achieve several firsts. I would be the first black chief of our department, I would be the youngest chief, and I would be the first paramedic to become chief. I agreed to accept the challenge and to work with the director chief to prepare for the position. But I also knew it would require much sacrifice on my part even to be considered for this position, let alone allowed to ascend to it. But with any sacrifices we make, it takes commitment, which will cost us sooner or later.

Two weeks later, I received a phone call from the chief. It was Thanksgiving, and I was out of town visiting my in-laws. He told me that my first task was to go to work at the Office of Emergency Management (OEM). I wondered, *Do I have to leave the fire department?* I asked him when I should prepare to leave, and he said, "Immediately." He wanted me to go to the OEM to raise my knowledge and understanding so I could learn more about how Nashville's infrastructure works. He knew that I needed to get out of my comfort zone and experience more areas other than the fire department.

I realized the director chief didn't have to help to prepare me, but I also knew that times were changing. He understood that to take the department to the next level, I needed to be well-prepared to excel, and he believed in my abilities to do that. I trusted his plan to prepare me to be the next chief, but I prayed about the direction he was leading me because I had no interest in going to the OEM. I was committed to the overall goal of rising through the ranks, but some of the tasks assigned to me along the way made me pause.

Ultimately, I agreed to move to the OEM not because it was what I wanted, but because I trusted the chief's vision. I understood that this move would align with one of my long-term goals of becoming more knowledgeable, and this new experience aligned with his vision. The change included a few small perks and incentives

I would get a six-percent raise and a company vehicle. That sounded like a fair bonus, but the move was not without its pitfalls. Some challenges I faced made me continue to question if I was going in the right direction. I started to count the cost, and I wasn't sure if it was worth it. It seemed that what I was sacrificing was bigger than I could have ever imagined.

First, although I was given a raise, I would have to give up a part-time job that guaranteed me almost $40,000 in extra income, which meant I had to completely restructure my family's finances. Second, at the OEM, I was a fish out of water. I didn't know anything, and the reputation I had built over the years meant nothing because no one knew who I was or what I could do. So, I would have to put in a lot of work and prove myself all over again.

I imagined people were wondering, *What is Will Swann doing? Is he rubbing shoulders with the wrong people just so he can climb the ladder?* And I discovered that there were people I had assumed would be in my corner but who became naysayers. Some days, it felt as if I was on an island by myself.

I was starting to think I had made a mistake, but I had given my word that I would take this path. I had to see it through. I needed to shut out all the noise and focus on the task, learn the position, get to know new people, and figure out what it took to make the OEM work successfully.

I would like to say that after giving it my best effort, it was all upward from there, but that's not the case. After a year, I was miserable. Although I was focused, ready to learn new skills, and committed to the task, things weren't working out the way I thought they should, and I made mistakes. But even in the darkest of clouds, there may be a silver lining.

Despite the setbacks and mistakes, I was growing, gaining experience, and getting better at my job. I was learning Nashville's infrastructure from the outside in. The adversity I faced made me better and more capable of understanding how things work in the Nashville Metropolitan government.

And just when I thought I had it all figured out, the chief called to give me devastating news. He told me that because of budget crunches, he would have to take away the company vehicle and my raise. I knew it wasn't what he wanted for me, but by that time, I knew I wasn't at the OEM for the financial and material benefits. If that was all it was about, I wouldn't have stayed there. Besides, I had sacrificed a lot more to make the move initially.

I assured the chief that I knew what the goal was, that it wouldn't be easy, but that I was committed to seeing it through. I thought of that setback as merely a bump in the road, and I was willing to persevere and move on.

The Reverend Dr. Martin Luther King Jr. talked about how people are not measured by their work when things are going well. Instead, they're measured by their work when things aren't going well and they're struggling. Can you smile, keep your head up, and be committed to finishing what you've started? Can you still believe in the purpose and the vision?

I believed I could be successful, and I stayed committed despite the problems I encountered. I went from being a captain to a district chief to a commander to the chief of staff to the chief of the department.

To be transparent, I admit that none of those promotions came without struggles and adversity, but the important takeaway is that I didn't focus just on a single situation. If I had done that, my motivation would have been as up and down as a roller coaster. Instead, I focused on my end goals. My commitment was not so much to a single task, but it was to the long-term vision, which made the individual tasks doable.

A Tool for Effective Leadership

We need tools that will help us excel, grow, and be successful. Commitment is one of those tools. It's not a quality that can be seen merely by looking at a person. Instead, commitment is proven through the work a person does. It requires action and effort, not just talk and empty promises. Many of us fall into the trap of saying how committed we are without rolling up our sleeves and putting in any sweat equity behind what we say. As writer and philosopher Jean-Paul Sartre said, "Commitment is an act, not a word."

Dr. Robert Hamm describes committed leaders as those who understand their influence on the behavior of those they lead, accept responsibility, invest in their work, can make tough decisions, give a consistent and clear message, regularly evaluate progress, and hold others accountable for progress.[1] As you can see, commitment and responsibility go hand in hand, and your willingness to take on this amount of dedication will determine your future success or failure.

Being committed can feel as if you're working without a Plan B, without a safety net, if things don't go the way you'd like. Not having a backup plan means you're "all in," totally dedicated to the path you're on. You're not constantly scanning the horizon for other options. Instead, you're determined to see a course through to completion.

And it's in the crucible of leadership where you learn how committed you are. When you set out to achieve your goals, you will be given tasks you will not want to take on. You will be given assignments that don't seem to be related to your desired outcomes. But this is where your dedication and commitment will be thoroughly tested and forged. You will be challenged every day, and these challenges will make you question your every decision.

Effective leaders know how to use commitment not just for personal goal-setting and achievement but to show the people they lead that they are serious about what they're doing. Your commitment draws people to you, and other people are inspired by your long-term quest for success and excellence. They will see your work ethic, your values, and your vision. Your commitment creates momentum and gives your organization strength.

You can be an example of commitment to people in your circle, showing them that they, too, can persevere through adversity and reap the benefits of not giving up. A long-term commitment will give you and the people you lead time to learn more, take risks, and succeed and fail while discovering best practices.

Every leader must have purpose and drive, just like the most successful athletes. For example, Michael Jordan is considered to be one of the greatest professional basketball players of all time. His dedication to the game and his work ethic showcased his commitment and made him a winning player. People like to win, and most people can't win if they aren't committed to what they're doing.

Jordan's dedication helped to win games for the Chicago Bulls and gained millions of fans. While most people didn't know Jordan personally, they knew what he brought to the arena when he played, and he was able to create a brand based solely on that. During one game, he even played through a bout of food poisoning. So strong was his commitment to the game that it transcended his concern for his physical health.

Jordan said he played the way he did because of first impressions, which mean everything. If someone saw him play for the first time, he wanted that person to see the best version of himself. He wanted to play at 100 percent in every game, and he wanted the fans to feel they had gotten their money's worth. That sentiment has stayed with me and echoes how I feel about being committed to my career and the people I lead.

As a leader, you get one shot to show people what you're made of, no matter what your profession is. When you're dedicated, it shows in your attitude as well as in your actions. People will be motivated and inspired by your faithfulness, and that will spur them to use your example to be more committed in their own lives. Evangelist Myles Monroe once said, "You don't become the person you wish to become; you become the person you choose to become. True leadership does not come through wishes; it comes by choices!"

Through Adversity and Pain

How can you honor your promises and stay on track when you're confronted with adversity? What should you do when you feel as if you've hit a wall? How do you balance praise on one hand and criticism on the other?

In leadership, this is when you're most under the microscope, and people will question why you're making certain moves. This is when you'll discover the doubters and naysayers who are just waiting for you to fail. As I examine my career trajectory, I can think of many instances of receiving the highest accolades at the same time I was receiving my harshest criticism.

For example, I received an award for the work I did during the Christmas Day bombing in downtown Nashville in 2020. But while I was being lauded for my leadership during that crisis, I was also being severely criticized for not promoting enough women in the fire department. I have never been against promoting women, but news stories portrayed me as sexist and took many things out of context to make that point.

At times like this, you can feel misunderstood and alone. You will need to make decisions that other people don't understand, and you will feel as if you're alone in your convictions. I could have allowed the false news reports to demoralize and depress me. No one likes to be on the bad end of a news story. Instead, I was still committed to my vision for the department.

I went back to work even though I was supposed to have been on vacation. I put on my best uniform, squared my shoulders, and put a smile on my face. I showed up with my head held high because I am secure in who I am, and I'm sure of the excellence of my work. I'm not a perfect man, but I have nothing to be ashamed of.

We all deal with extremes in life. One day, we're celebrating a baby being born; the next day, we're mourning the loss of a parent. Or just as a husband is happy about a job promotion, he comes home to find out his wife has been laid off. The Bible talks about these extremes and tells us that there's a time for all things (Ecclesiastes 3), some of them quite adverse and unpleasant. But that shouldn't shake our faith or our commitment to the assignment we've been given.

When my daughter passed away, it was extremely devastating because no parent wants to have to bury a child. I am the chief of the Nashville Fire Department, but that doesn't shield me from personal loss. I have to deal with work, but I also have to be present for my family as they, too, deal with the loss.

Life doesn't stop because of adversity and pain. I still have to solve problems at work and at home. People are depending on me to be there for them. It's in these moments when I must be intentional. Under this enormous pressure, I might want to hide in a closet, put my head down, and avoid life; but I don't have that luxury as a husband, a father, a leader, or a child of God.

In being intentional, I'm telling myself and those I lead that I'm committed to the vision and that I'm going to dig deeper and do whatever it takes to stay on track. But my commitment is not formed in a vacuum. The apostle Paul admonished the church to prepare itself for adversity: "Therefore take up the whole armor of God, so that you may be able to withstand on that evil day, and having done everything, *to stand firm*" (Ephesians 6:13, NRSV, italics added).

My faith in God and my values strengthen me at times like these. I can stand strong because God anchors me when everything is in chaos. Whether I'm dealing with the death of a loved one or with dishonest reports about my work, I can stay focused and committed.

Becoming a Committed Leader

If you're new to leadership, you may wonder if you have the level of commitment you need to succeed. Ask yourself the following questions:

- What am I willing to do to succeed?
- Can I give 100 percent every time I'm called on to complete a task even when I don't like what I'm asked to do?
- Can I be dedicated to my goals through adversity, personal loss, criticism, doubts, and fears?

If you answered no to any of these questions, you have work to do to raise and strengthen your level of commitment. Or perhaps it's time to reevaluate what you're doing and decide if you should change course. If you're not convinced of the overall vision, then you're wasting your time.

Your level of commitment will often determine the decisions you make. You will value the things you're committed to, and you'll discard or abandon the things to which you're not committed. This will save you precious time, energy, and resources, which you can best employ doing something of value. If every time you start to work on something you're filled with dread, perhaps you're not committed to it. If you can't stay focused on the goals and vision you've mapped out, then your level of commitment is not what it should be.

But don't confuse zeal or passion with commitment. It's appropriate to be excited about your vision, a new project, or your organization's mission. But zeal and passion often ebb and flow depending on your mood or what you're currently facing. Just make sure you understand the difference between interests and commitments. Your interests will change and are dependent on your circumstances to pursue them. However, the commitments you make require you to be all in, no matter what is going on around you.

Your interests can also lead you to give your allegiance to causes that may not be appropriate for your leadership. That's when you must pay attention to your moral and ethical compass and allow it to guide you. When I'm faced with an ethical dilemma, I ask myself, *Is this right or wrong? Should I stay with this although it may cause hardship?* I'm not talking about avoiding struggles and sacrifice just to make life easier. Instead, I'm saying that your commitment to a cause or a goal shouldn't cause unnecessary hardship and collateral pain for others, and you need to find your limit.

There will come a time when you need to concede that you've gone as far as you can in one area. It's okay to admit when you've reached your limit. Perhaps you find you're not maintaining a good work/life balance or that you're overcommitted, which ultimately will make you, the people you lead, and other people in your life miserable.

It's sometimes difficult to be courageous enough to bow out or walk away. I may think I'm hitting a home run at work. I'm Chief William Swann, and people respond to that with deference. They open doors for me. They drive me where I need to go. But what good is all that when I go home and my wife isn't happy or my children are ashamed to call me Dad? That's when I know my commitment has gone off the rails, and I need to reevaluate and refocus.

It's a delicate balance, and leaders—me included—have sometimes gotten it wrong. A quick way to check your commitment level and determine whether it's balanced is to look at your bank account and your calendar. This will show you where you spend most of your money and your time. How do you allocate your time? Is there a balance of it spent at home, at work, and in the community? Where do you spend your money? Do you spend on things, people, and organizations that offer value for your money? We need to keep our lives as balanced as possible, understanding what's important and where we're needed most.

As you mature in your leadership, be careful that you don't build up one area of your life while neglecting others. You should nourish your spiritual life, make sure your family is taken care of, and honor your work commitments, but also set aside time to take care of yourself so you can keep everything in balance. You may be able to pretend for a while that everything is okay, but over time, being out of alignment and unbalanced will make you an ineffective leader.

I've seen this happen to many people in leadership. I've worked alongside brilliant people who seemed to have it all together, only to find out they were on the verge of divorce or were suffering from depression. You need to strike this balance and not make commitments that will become impossible burdens. If you experience burnout or become overloaded, you aren't doing yourself, your family, your community, or your organization any favors.

If you are concerned about your dedication and commitment, now is the time to level up. You should work to develop commitment as one of your leadership tools. So, consider the following tips:[2]

- **Be patient as you develop your commitment.** It often grows steadily but slowly. Don't rush headlong into anything and pledge your allegiance to it before you know more. Give yourself time.

- **Don't guilt-trip yourself or other people into commitment.** You won't get the long-term results you want. You and the people you lead want to feel that you're involved in meaningful work. If that's the case, it's okay to contribute in different but meaningful ways. You can be proud when you invite people to be committed to your organization. You're not imposing on them; you're offering them something of value.

- **Instead of shutting down people you don't agree with, try to work through conflict.** The richness of diversity of thought is valuable, and working through differences with colleagues and those you lead will pay dividends.

- **Overcome personal and professional obstacles.** Decide that you won't be defeated by your struggles, pain, criticism, adversity, or loss. When you come out on the other side of these situations, you should see growth and recognize how much your senses, wisdom, and discernment have sharpened.

- **Hold your colleagues and those you lead to high principles.** Hold one another accountable for staying on track and being committed to the vision. Sometimes all you need to keep going is a nudge from someone else or a warning word that you're out of balance.

- **Challenge one another to take the next step.** Next steps can be scary because they're unknown, and fear can consume you when you aren't sure what's next.

Encouraging your team members, or allowing others to encourage you, can go a long way in building your organization for the future.

- **Learn from mistakes and setbacks.** Glean from these opportunities as much knowledge as you can. Don't waste them by wallowing in self-pity and bitterness.

I'm also inspired by the writings of John Maxwell and Jim Collins on the levels of commitment in leadership. John Neufeld, a trainer for ACHIEVE Center for Leadership and Workplace Performance, lists those levels as:[3]

- **Level 1: Position (Rights).** People follow you because they have to. Many times, this is how we first begin in leadership. People who stay at this level often devalue others, feed on politics, and place their rights over their responsibilities.

- **Level 2: Permission (Relationships).** People follow you because they want to. They follow because you care about them, are encouraging, and practice the golden rule.

- **Level 3: Production (Results).** People follow you because of what you have done for the organization. By following you, the team gets things done and ultimately achieves positive results.

- **Level 4: People Development (Reproduction).** People follow you because of what you have done for them.

The goal of leadership is to develop leaders, not gain followers. People at Level 4 create a leadership culture. They realize that developing leaders is a life commitment, not a job commitment.

- **Level 5: The Pinnacle (Respect).** People follow because of who you are and what you represent. Level-5 leaders remain humble and teachable, maintain core focus, and create the right inner circle to keep them grounded. They do what only they can do and develop top leaders.

What level are you willing to commit to? Every level brings more commitment, but it also involves more sacrifice.

To be effective, you need to accept that struggle and sacrifice are part of your journey, but that shouldn't stop you from being committed to what you do. You should want to show those you lead the best version of yourself, give 100 percent every single time, and aspire to a higher level of commitment with more responsibility. Sometimes the sacrifices will cost you a lot, but they should still be balanced with the other areas of your life and not a waste of time and energy.

As the saying goes, "BS might take you to the top, but it won't keep you there." It might be easy to bluff your way to the higher levels in your career and certain networking circles, but sooner or later, people will see through you—and it's a long fall from the top! Instead of trying to take shortcuts, be committed to doing things the right way. It won't be easy, but it will be more sustainable. Sometimes you will face great adversity beyond what you think you can withstand, but that's when you'll need to dig in a little deeper and be intentional about what decisions you make next to stay at the top.

A lot has happened in Nashville since I stepped into my role as chief of the fire department, but I've shown up every day and put the department in the best light possible. I've been rewarded for my success, and my decisions have been scrutinized and criticized. But my commitment and sense of duty, even in the face of adversity, have made me valuable and have created a sense of trust and respect.

"Commitment requires hard work in the heat of the day; it requires faithful exertion in behalf of chosen purposes and the enhancement of chosen values."
John Gardner

Chapter Two

Confidence

Along my leadership journey, I've learned to be prepared for life's experiences, no matter what they are. During my time in the United States Army, I was trained to develop strategies to meet adversity head-on. But it's difficult to be adequately prepared without confidence in my training, my abilities, and myself.

But most people are probably not born bold and ready to take on the world. Many of us struggle with insecurities around who we are and our mental and physical abilities. Developing a healthy level of confidence occurs in phases, and we draw from different people and experiences to grow and maintain it. When people ask me how I can be so secure in who I am, I share with them two main sources of confidence: my family and my faith.

My parents, Arthur and Darcus Swann, raised me and my siblings in a small Southwestern Virginia coal mining town where racism was no stranger. While my parents did not teach us to hate anyone, they did tell us that to succeed we would have to work twice as hard to get ahead. They told us, "Because of who you are, be the best at what you do in everything. And if you're doing something, you make sure you do it to excellence. Make yourself valuable so it doesn't matter what you look like."

My parents' wise words instilled in me a spirit of excellence that I could apply to everything I planned to do, which strengthened and increased my confidence. And I would need it when I later faced racism in the military and the communities of Nashville, my adopted hometown.

I've read in the Bible about many men and women who served God. But one thing Adam, Noah, Abraham, Sarah, David, Peter, Paul, and many other biblical heroes had in common is that they weren't perfect. But despite their imperfections and flaws, God chose to partner with them in His plan for humanity. It's not their perfection that God wanted; it was their confidence in Him. And that's another reason why I have a greater capacity to lead and serve in my community.

Throughout my career, I've experienced disappointments and failures, but I keep going. Instead of giving up, I go back to the basics and shore up the foundation of my faith and my vision for the future. Then I begin to rebuild what my mistakes or the mistakes of others have destroyed.

Confidence Is Critical

Among many other important qualities, confidence may often be overlooked; but I don't know anyone who wants to follow a person who is weak, insecure, full of doubt, and self-loathing. Such a leader wouldn't be a good example of success or be able to impart much of a vision to those who are following. So it's important to strike a realistic balance between confidence and humility.

Sometimes, we may rely more on our education and training in a myriad of subjects to make leadership easier. We may believe that the more knowledge we have the more likely that everything in our world will simply fall into place. While there's nothing wrong with education and knowledge, they're not sustainable in the long term. Despite our wealth of knowledge on any given subject, if we don't have the confidence to back it up, we will struggle and eventually fail to be good leaders.

Many experts believe that confidence is so critical that it determines everything else, and a lack of it will undermine everything we do. Insecurity nullifies my leadership and makes it difficult for me to gain trust. We may be trained to be effective and efficient in many areas, but without confidence, our efforts will be in vain.

Columnist Francisco Dao wrote, "Self-confidence is the fundamental basis from which leadership grows. Trying to teach leadership without first building confidence is like building a house on a foundation of sand. It may have a nice coat of paint, but it is ultimately shaky at best. While the leadership community has focused on passion, communication, and empowerment, they've ignored this most basic element and, in the process, they have planted these other components of leadership in a bed of quicksand."[1]

Dao confirms my belief that a confident person is more effective. Without that component, a person will find his or her journey difficult and fraught with disappointment and failures. Every challenge—and there will be many—will be met with fear instead of boldness. People who disagree with or doubt a leader's direction will be able to usurp power and control an organization because the leader isn't confident enough to stand in his or her convictions. Confidence is essential to long-term viability and success.

Confidence vs. Arrogance

Most of us have known people who irritated us with their arrogance. They may have thought they were displaying a healthy level of confidence; instead, they made grand claims about their abilities that they never quite seemed to live up to: the cocky guy on the football team who thought he was going to crush the competition but ended up on the bench at the beginning of the season; the coworker who padded her resume thinking that would make her more likely to get promoted only to find that she's struggling to keep up with everyone else because she's not qualified for the position she has or for the promotion she wants.

Arrogant people may appear confident on the outside, but often they're hiding behind a thin veneer of self-deception. If they have any achievements, they're ruined by a sense of superiority and self-importance. But many times, arrogant people are exposed for their insecurities and bogus claims. We can't afford to be arrogant or overconfident. Effective leaders have to walk in humility not because they are weak or incapable, but because they understand that being secure in oneself is not an opportunity to get too caught up in successes.

Leadership often takes us down rough, rocky paths; and despite our best-laid plans, there is always the potential for missteps and failures. Confidence keeps us going whether we're succeeding and celebrating our victories or whether we're being challenged and facing adversity. But great leaders don't allow their self-assurance to cause them to become haughty and self-righteous. They aren't open to learning from their mistakes and will continue to fail.

As a Christian, I strive to be more like Jesus Christ. During His earthly ministry, He could have proven His power by killing His enemies and avoiding His crucifixion. Even some of His disciples thought He had come to set up a kingdom on earth, to upset the government of Rome, and to show His power over His enemies. But Jesus didn't have an identity crisis, and He didn't have to prove anything. He knew exactly who He was: the Son of God. Instead, He used His power to teach, heal, and deliver those who followed Him. He never allowed His power to make Him arrogant.

Like Jesus, I endeavor to walk in humility instead of arrogance. However, as a human being, I realize that I'm not all-powerful. I am not who I am simply because of what I alone bring to the table. I've had the strong and loving support of many people along the way. For example, my parents gave me a foundation of excellence and faith upon which I've been able to build a healthy level of confidence that has allowed me to confront life's obstacles, as well as those problems unique to leadership.

If I had allowed arrogance to overwhelm me, I doubt I would have been successful in my journey from soldier to firefighter to the first African American chief of the Nashville Fire Department. Perhaps arrogance would have propelled me to this position, but it wouldn't have kept me here. I would have lost much-needed support from family members, friends, and colleagues; and I have relied on those persons who have been kind and gracious enough to walk alongside me every step of the way. Arrogance would have killed those relationships and would have contributed to my downfall.

Confidence vs. Insecurity

Just as a leader can't be arrogant or overconfident, he or she can't be plagued with insecurities or overwhelmed with self-doubt either. Because I've been trained to overcome obstacles, learned from the wealth and wisdom of other people's knowledge and experiences, and held fast to my faith, I trust my abilities. I'm certain that I can lead and serve others and succeed in achieving goals that move us closer to our shared vision.

I've been confronted with people who didn't like me or trust me because I'm African American, or they doubted my leadership because they didn't bother to get to know who I am and what I can do. In those cases, I had two choices: I could give up because the people around me didn't believe I was up to the task, or I could be confident in who I am and what I know I can do and be certain that I indeed possess the power to be effective. I'm aware of my abilities and trust them even if some people I've encountered don't share that trust.

Being confident has helped me to develop critical thinking skills. If I were insecure, I would just go along to get along. I would follow the groupthink of the moment. But that would destroy me as a leader. I must be able to think independently and question visions, strategies, and outcomes. I must put aside my biases and emotional responses so that I can make sound decisions. I can't do that if my thinking is too small or wholly dependent on what other people are saying. I'm confident in my discernment and experiences that if something doesn't seem right or seems to be unjust, then I need to ask questions and find out what is going on.

Only arrogant or insecure people go with the status quo every time because "we've always done it this way." I have to use data and facts instead of simply relying on the traditions of the organization. A lack of confidence to make good decisions and a lack of critical thinking will keep leaders and those they lead bogged down in time-wasting meetings, useless training sessions, and outdated policies. Instead, great leaders explore why things are done in a certain way and look for better, more efficient ways to achieve their goals.

Insecure people also may be afraid of what they might find, or perhaps they're afraid they may be exposed for not knowing everything. I'm confident enough to admit I don't always have all the answers. But I'm bold and assertive enough in my thinking that I'll do my best to find out what I need to know.

I want to be a confident leader, but I also want to cultivate confidence in the people who follow my lead, which is a twofold process. First, I want to earn their trust. I want them to believe that when I make decisions, I have their best interest at heart, and my decisions are sound and will take us to the next level. I know that it's more difficult to earn people's trust if I'm indecisive and insecure.

We live in a cynical age, and many of the people we lead don't respect authority "no matter what." So I know that every day, I'm working to earn and maintain the trust of those I lead. They're watching me not only to see if I have a lapse of judgment but, more importantly, how I handle it. Most people understand that we're all human and that we make mistakes, even the greatest leaders. It's how we deal with those mistakes that can make or break their confidence in us.

Second, I want to help those I lead to cultivate their confidence. They may not be following me forever. Someday, they may step out of my shadow and become leaders in their own right. So, I want them to be well-prepared for that day. Just as my mentors have done with me, I want to have the insight and knowledge to see their potential and help them build their confidence and self-esteem in a healthy way and avoid arrogance and insecurity. I want them to have all the tools they'll need to be great leaders.

Being confident has helped me to be positive about the future, knowing I can take risks and come out on top. Having this mindset has emboldened me to move forward in the face of doubt, not back away from it.

Becoming a Confident Leader

If you're going to be a successful leader, you won't build up your confidence by accident. You will need to be intentional. When people want to strengthen their bodies and build up muscle, they go to a gym or develop an exercise regimen at home that will work their muscles and make their bodies stronger. The results don't happen overnight, and they don't happen by sitting in front of the computer or the TV all day.

Building up confidence works in a similar way. You will need to be intentional in everything you do. You will need to work to build up and strengthen your confidence. You won't see any results if you refuse to leave the safety of your comfort zone, but you will see gradual results as you work to change your mindset and your actions. To take your confidence to the next level, I encourage you to begin with the following steps:

Build a strong support system. Ultimately, developing your confidence is your responsibility, but you won't be able to do it by yourself. You will need trusted people who believe in you and your potential and want to see you succeed. They will be crucial to helping you become a more confident person, so don't discount where this support might come from. It might be your parents or other family members, friends, employers or coworkers, mentors, and people with whom you've networked.

My director chief saw my potential in becoming chief of the department. He had a vision and took steps to help me reach that goal. Though circumstances didn't always work out as we had planned, his confidence in my potential helped me to believe that I would ascend to the position I'm in today.

Poet John Donne wrote, "No man is an island, entire of itself. Every man is a piece of the continent, a part of the main." And I'll add to that: You won't get far if you're trying to be The Lone Ranger. There's a time to stand on your own, but there's also a time to lean on those who can help you improve and become the best version of yourself that you can be.

When you have a strong and supportive network, you have the resources to draw upon when you need them, especially when you're facing adversity. These relationships will build self-confidence because you will know that you're not going it alone. They also provide you with critical feedback that can help your character to become stronger. The people in your support network can be vital and valuable resources in your leadership journey.

Get out of your comfort zone. It's human nature to want to be comfortable and safe, but great and awesome things are usually not accomplished by staying in your comfort zone. Playing it safe doesn't give you the experiences you will need to learn and grow. And if you're not growing, learning, and stretching yourself in new ways, you will feel incredibly exposed when you confront life's realities and things don't go to plan.

The desire to be safe is also a trait shared by insecure persons and those who are arrogant. Both types of people are closed off to new experiences and believe there is nothing new for them to learn. To open themselves to anything new would take them outside of their safe space and into the unknown, which for them is frightening. They can no longer control their environment and are unsure of next steps, and this behavior doesn't make for effective leadership.

Staying safe usually means change will be more difficult. There's one thing we know for certain: Change is inevitable. It happens to all of us. But people stuck in their comfort zones fight change and abhor progress, which is why they are often left behind and desperately out of touch. Insecure leaders don't want the challenges and uncertainties of new paths. They'll never be trailblazers or mavericks in their organizations because not having all the answers frightens them into becoming stagnant.

But confident people embrace the unknown because they can be assured that they have what it takes to navigate it. You don't have to take a flying leap all at once out of your comfort zone. It's okay to take baby steps at first. You might stumble a bit in the beginning; but for each small step away from safety that you take, you will feel that much more confident in your abilities.

Before long, you'll be taking long strides, knowing that as you go, you're developing your skills, drawing on more resources, building your faith, and confronting adversity. In other words, you are becoming more comfortable with being uncomfortable. Facing the unknown and solving problems become easier, and you'll see your confidence grow.

Be authentic. There's nothing more damaging to an organization than a leader who is not genuine. The people you lead are looking for transparency and honesty. We no longer live in a world where people want to blindly follow a hierarchy of people they don't know and don't have access to. Technology and 24-hour news coverage have made a somewhat level playing field and made our world feel much smaller than in the past. Leaders are exposed, and people feel entitled to question their decisions.

Those who don't adopt an authentic mindset haven't developed confidence. They may be hiding behind a façade of arrogance, thinking that will cover them until they figure it out. But to be a great leader, you can't afford to be anything less than authentic. The people you lead and the communities you serve need you to be your best, and they will eventually see through you for who you are. So, you need to be authentically confident and prepared for whatever you're going to face.

According to management expert Dan McCarthy, there are other key steps you can take in developing confidence. **First, learn as much as you can about leadership.** Don't assume you know everything you need to know. Study books, watch videos, talk with other leaders, and "learn what leaders do and don't do. Learn the frameworks, tools and skills required to lead. The more you know about a subject, including leadership, the more confident you'll be."

Second, be realistically self-aware. Know your strengths, but be strong enough to receive constructive criticism so you will understand where you need to improve. **Third, help others and then celebrate your wins.** Leadership is about engaging with others, but some people are so focused on their own track to success, that they forget about the people they lead. Have a more other-focused approach to leadership. And then when you and those you lead have victories, celebrate. "This isn't about tooting your own horn, it's about getting into the habit of looking for and recognizing the wins of others."

Finally, stop asking for permission, and make a decision. "Confident leaders would rather ask for forgiveness than permission and are comfortable making decisions without having 100 percent certainty."[2] The people we lead want us to be decisive, not overanalyze everything or become easily overwhelmed by making decisions. In other words, don't have "analysis paralysis."

It's impossible to know every variable that you'll encounter when you decide to go in one direction or the other, but great leaders make room for their mistakes. They know that these mistakes will inform what they do next and can be leveraged as opportunities to correct course and make better choices next time.

Being confident doesn't come naturally to all of us. Many of us, through trial and error, have forged new levels of confidence we didn't think we could achieve. But we did the work and built up our confidence. We drew from the resources we had at our disposal and learned from those who offered their support and wisdom. And we have positioned ourselves to be successful.

If I'd stopped growing when people doubted me or after making mistakes, I'd never be where I am today. I've learned just as much, if not more, from my mistakes as I have from my successes. I turned people's doubt into a catalyst to propel me forward, and I've turned challenges and difficulties into opportunities to learn and grow, even when those obstacles seemed insurmountable.

My encounters with racism, criticism, doubt, negativity, and adversity have motivated me instead of making me bitter. Instead of conceding and retreating, I've used every bit of those negative experiences to boost my confidence and sharpen my skills. I rely on the solid foundation provided by my family and the confidence in my ability to succeed. Also, my faith in God and myself has been stretched, strengthened, and solidified and has made me more confident and effective. And I want to pay that forward to others.

> *"You have to have confidence in your ability,*
> *and then be tough enough to follow through."*
> *Former First Lady Rosalynn Carter*

Integrity

Integrity matters. As many leadership experts attest, integrity remains one of the most important qualities we can have. But as with many good qualities, integrity is developed over time with plenty of work to improve ourselves. As we mature and fine-tune our moral compass, we should make integrity an essential part of who we are. If we skimp on integrity, we damage our influence, lose our ability to cast vision, and destroy our destiny. That's why we must work on being honest and trustworthy.

I have looked to family members, mentors, and other prominent people who model the essential characteristics of leadership. My parents were my first teachers as they instilled in me a firm grip on my faith, a desire for excellence, and the importance of hard work. I wouldn't be the man I am without their guidance. In addition to my parents, I have benefited from the examples of other people who have had a profound effect on me. They have made a difference in their communities and the wider world.

One such person is the late Nelson Mandela, former president of South Africa. As an activist in the fight against apartheid, he made it his life's work to advocate for freedom and social justice, and he paid a heavy price.

He was imprisoned for over 27 years. For his Herculean efforts involving peacemaking, he was awarded the Nobel Peace Prize.

I am inspired by Mandela's leadership because he was uncompromising, even when his freedom was on the line. When he became president, he focused on unity among different factions instead of further dividing the nation and seeking retribution. He also kept his promise to step down after completing a single five-year term in office, showing his humility.

When I look at the life of Nelson Mandela, I see a legacy of honor and integrity. He was a selfless man who dedicated his life to the cause of freedom. Although he was imprisoned for his activism, he held to his belief in justice and inclusion for everyone. I'm challenged by his example. As a Christian, a husband, a father, a director chief, and a friend, I have to evaluate my integrity and discover if I have what it takes to stand in the face of adversity. Can I hold firm to my faith and my values, even when society doesn't like me or agree with me? Am I a man of integrity? Will I leave a legacy of faith and honor for the next generations?

Mandela once said, "A bright future beckons. The onus is on us, through hard work, honesty and integrity, to reach for the stars." His was the type of leadership that I want to model and mentor for those I lead and serve. I want to carry forth that hope for the future and be a man of integrity. I never met President Mandela, but his influential leadership transcends the borders of South Africa, and his vision for the future goes beyond the era immediately after the abolition of apartheid.

When Mandela said, "It's in your hands now," he was passing the torch to the next generations to shape the future, and that call is to all who want to be agents of change whether it's at home, in their organizations, in their churches, in their communities, or in the global public square.

I'm thankful to those persons who have been examples of integrity in their work and their personal lives. Most of them weren't leaders on the world stage like Nelson Mandela. Many of the persons who have blazed the trails before me were regular men and women who had families, went to work, attended church, taught school, coached teams, and tried to make the world better in their own small ways. Many of them may have never guessed that they were guiding lights for those of us who have benefited from their influence, but the impact of their lives has been huge. And I'm working to follow in their footsteps and be an example of integrity and faithfulness.

The Intersection of Integrity

Many people define *integrity* as "doing the right thing, even when no one is looking." While that is the core of what integrity is, I believe it's more than that. Integrity, especially for leaders, intersects with many of the key characteristics we need to be successful.

Doing the right thing alone is not enough. Dishonest, immoral people will often do the right thing for selfish or unethical reasons. People donate millions of dollars to good causes not because they want to help others, but perhaps they can write it off on their taxes or because they have been promised buildings will be built and named after them. People also do good things to provide a smoke-screen to hide the not-so-good things they're doing. They want to present themselves as upstanding, morally good people, but their motives tell another story.

So there must be more to it than just doing the right thing. My integrity has to be sustainable when there's not necessarily anything in it for me, when I may not get anything in return. It must be built on a foundation of ethics and morals provided by my faith, and it has to intersect with honesty, trustworthiness, responsibility, accountability, and consistency.

Integrity is not a bargaining chip that I can use for leverage. No one is going to believe that I am honorable if I'm honest in one area but dishonest about everything else. Those who follow me will be paying attention to my track record. If they don't believe that I'm the man I claim to be, they won't trust me, and they won't follow me for long.

I'm not saying that leaders never make mistakes. Unfortunately, many people believe we are infallible, we don't mess up, we have no problems, and we should never fail. This mindset is a recipe for disaster. Leaders and those who follow us will be disappointed because we will eventually make mistakes, proving that we are human and fallible.

No leader is perfect and will make mistakes along the way. But people with integrity will take responsibility and work to make things right not because they get caught, but because they want to be honest. Paul stated in 1 Corinthians 15:10, "But by the grace of God I am what I am, and his grace to me was not without effect. No, I worked harder than all of them—yet not I, but the grace of God that was with me."

Paul was a man with a virtually flawless pedigree. He was educated by the best scholars of his day, and he had dual citizenship in Tarsus and Rome, which gave him unique privileges. He led three missionary journeys to start churches and support Christians throughout the ancient world, but he recognized that he could not be the man he was without the grace of God. I've achieved many things in my life, but like Paul, I know that I would not be who I am without God's extravagant grace and mercy.

Great leaders are not just vocal about what they get right; they also own their humanity and their flaws. In this way, leaders, as well as those who follow them, can learn from their mistakes. Transparency isn't just for putting our good deeds in the spotlight. It shines a light on mistakes, too. But great leaders don't fear accountability and ownership of their mistakes. They welcome the opportunity to learn from them.

These leaders have set higher standards for themselves than anyone else, and they live by those standards, along with their values. Not only do they want to model the right behavior, but they also want integrity to be an essential part of their identity, of who they are. People who are watching leaders with integrity will expect "the talk to match the walk." They want us to honor our word and keep our promises. They want leaders to have to play by the same rules as everyone else and not create an elite system that allows us to play by different rules.

Integrity Is a Choice

In his book *Uncommon: Finding Your Path to Significance*, former football coach Tony Dungy wrote, "Integrity, the choice between what's convenient and what's right."[1] Throughout his long and successful career, Coach Dungy won many games and rose to the top of his profession, but he's respected more for what he has done off the field than on.

Many of Dungy's colleagues and former players have been inspired by his integrity, and he has served as a role model, example, and mentor to many of them. His drive to make the right choices draws people to him, especially when they're seeking help and wise counsel.

Every day, all of us are presented with a myriad of choices. Depending on our careers or family life, we may have to make hundreds of choices each day. What we decide for any of those choices may have ripple effects that may change the course of our lives forever.

As chief of the fire department, I have to make choices that affect those I lead and the city we protect. When I'm faced with tough decisions, I have to view them through the lens of my faith. As a Christian, my life is strengthened by prayer and the truth of God's word, and when I build on these, integrity is interwoven throughout my life. When I'm weighing my decisions each day, I have to choose integrity every time if I'm going to be effective. I can't shrug off my responsibilities and not choose. As the saying goes, "Not making a choice is making a choice."

According to counselors Jeff and Terra Mattson, the key to being a successful leader is not about perfection, but it is "a commitment to shrinking the gap between the values you preach and live."[2] The Mattsons also emphasize that integrity is a way of life, not just a mask you wear when you show up for work and meet with employees or arrive at home and greet your family.[3] Integrity has to be essential to who you are and what your life is about.

We don't become people of integrity by accident. Developing our character requires us to be intentional about the choices we make, such as choosing to be honest and not lie, no matter how harmless we think our lies may be; choosing to admit when we're wrong and work to make it right; and choosing to use caution when we're faced with adversity because it's during our worst times that we could make wrong choices that will affect the rest of our lives.[4]

Too many of us have known people who didn't choose integrity. We've worked for organizations, attended churches, or voted for politicians who pretended to be honorable and trustworthy only to leave us disappointed and emotionally scarred by their dishonesty. Since then, we've had emotional wounds that haven't healed, and we find it hard to trust persons in authority because we don't believe they deserve our trust, loyalty, and respect.

As unfortunate as those situations are, perhaps we can learn something from them. It should motivate and challenge us to be intentional in our choices and always choose integrity so that we can create positive experiences with those we lead.

Mutual Benefits

As leaders, we set the tone for our organizations. Persons in our circle of influence are looking to us for guidance, so when we operate without integrity, we create an atmosphere of distrust and dishonesty. It's difficult for anyone in our organization to be productive in such a corrosive environment.

I strive to cultivate a positive atmosphere. I know that when I model integrity and other leadership qualities, I'm presenting the best version of myself, but I also know that integrity in the workplace will produce mutual benefits. I'm encouraging those I lead to be their best selves so that we can do our greatest work together.

For every stage of my career, I've been aware that what I was called to do wasn't just for my benefit. I knew that if I set a good example from the beginning, everyone on the team would see growth.

It's challenging when we move from one position to another. We might believe that we should focus solely on ourselves, our careers, our brand, and how far up the ladder we can climb. But we are also forced to care for the needs of those we lead as much as for our own needs. If we strive for those mutual benefits, we can establish more effective leadership.

Becoming a Leader of Integrity

Do you lead with integrity? It's important to learn to be a person of integrity for yourself and those you lead. Without it, your leadership is in jeopardy. If you're not sure you're operating with integrity, ask yourself the following questions:[5]

- Am I accountable for my behavior and the decisions I make?
- Do I accept responsibility for my mistakes?
- Am I setting a good example for my direct reports?
- Do I always follow through on my commitments and promises?
- Do I act in ways that build trust with my direct reports?

Most of our characteristics, especially those that help us to become good leaders, are forged over time and with experience. Most of us don't just happen to be good leaders. We work at it as we learn and grow. This process helps us to develop our character.

What does it look like when integrity isn't present? We fail. We create a toxic environment of distrust. If you want to develop integrity, consider these steps:[6]

- **Model integrity.** Be a good example for those you lead at home, at work, and in your community; and avoid breaking the rules or taking shortcuts to get things done. When you ignore company policies, break the speed limit, play office politics, gossip about others, cheat on your spouse, excuse various addictions, and lie to get out of trouble, you're signaling to those you lead that these behaviors are appropriate. These are not the fruits of integrity, and you won't be able to leave a good legacy when you engage in these actions. Instead, every day, choose to be a person of integrity, and let people see behavior that is honest and honorable.

- **Take responsibility.** It's often difficult for us to take the blame when we make mistakes. Sometimes as leaders, we are put on pedestals, and many of those we lead hang on our every word. They may see us as superhumans. It's hard to tumble off that pedestal. But to be effective, we must live in the light and truth, not in darkness and shadows. Don't allow people to put you on a pedestal because when you mess up, you'll have a long way to fall. But if you stay humble and transparent, you'll be more accessible and more relatable. When you make mistakes, accept the blame, try to fix them, learn from them, and move forward.

- **Keep your promises.** Leaders possess great talents and skills, but we're not miracle workers. Often, we overpromise but underperform because we stretch ourselves too thin or we're trying to be all things to all people. Take a step back and reevaluate what you can realistically do. If you don't honor your word or keep your promises, those you lead will lose faith in you; and nothing ruins a reputation faster than when disgruntled coworkers, clients, family members, and neighbors spread the word that you're not reliable. Be honest, and then strive to do what you say you're going to do.

- **Develop a good reputation.** Speaking of reputations, it's in your best interest and the validity of your leadership to develop a good reputation at home, at work, at church, and in your community. Your reputation will often be the only currency you have in your relationships, especially with people you're meeting for the first time. Most of us have heard people say, "Your reputation precedes you." That's when we wonder if what has been said about us was good or bad. But if we've been intentional about cultivating a good reputation beyond reproach, then we don't have to worry about what someone has heard about us. Keep in mind that it may take years to build a good reputation, but it can be damaged by negative behavior in an instant.

- **Live up to your own high standards.** High standards don't have to be impossible, unrealistic goals. High standards should reflect your values, morals, and ethics. You have to think through your decisions and look at more than how you will benefit. Instead, think about how your decisions will affect your family, your organization, your church, and your community. Your integrity, or lack thereof, will always inform what you choose to do.

I've looked to various people who have effectively modeled integrity. From my parents to the Reverend Martin Luther King Jr. to President Nelson Mandela to other mentors and colleagues, I've incorporated their examples to build and strengthen my character. If we look closely, we can find many people around us who are men and women of integrity. We may not know them personally, but we can still learn from them and grow in our journey. When looking for honest and honorable people, don't overlook family members, teachers, spiritual and community leaders, and entrepreneurs.

How you define *integrity* is one aspect of how you develop as a leader. You may presently be hyperfocused on getting ahead in your career and grabbing that next promotion. Or at home, perhaps you're preoccupied with so many things at work or online that you've not been a good example to your spouse and your children. Think more intentionally about what integrity is and if you need to work harder to live it out. I've always believed that I can't be a good leader at home, at work, or in the community if I don't work to be better every day.

Among the many choices you'll make, being an honorable person is one of the most important. Integrity, or the lack thereof, will make or break your leadership. When it comes to leading others, we may not get another opportunity if we break the trust of those in our families and among those we lead. So always choose integrity no matter what. Don't allow money, position, power, or temptation to cloud your judgment.

Choosing integrity isn't always popular, especially if you are ambitious and want to get ahead. You probably know other people who have taken shortcuts and been unscrupulous to be successful.

Coach Dungy was right when he wrote that integrity often boils down to a choice between what's convenient and what's right. It may seem faster or easier to choose anything other than integrity because we see how other people seem to prosper when they choose to be unethical or dishonest. But don't let the poor decisions of others lead you down the wrong path. Stay the course, and choose integrity every time!

"Image is what people think we are.
Integrity is what we really are."
John C. Maxwell

Vision

I once heard a story that has helped me to think deeper about casting vision as a leader. It's about three bricklayers and their perspectives on their work. One day, an interested passerby asked each man the same question.

"What are you doing?"

The first bricklayer answered, "I'm a bricklayer, and I'm working hard laying bricks so I can feed my family."

"I'm a builder," said the second bricklayer, "and I'm building a wall."

The third bricklayer, the most productive of the three, said with a gleam in his eye, "I'm a cathedral builder, and I'm building a great cathedral to the Almighty."

This short, simple story holds a profound truth for me. Each bricklayer had a vision as to who he thought he was and what he wanted to build, and each man's perception of his identity and purpose became his reality.

Part of my life's work is to help those I lead to see themselves as "cathedral builders," to find their identity in a higher purpose than just laying bricks. I want to inspire others to have a clear vision of where they need to go and to discover meaning and purpose in their work along the way.

Political activist Lee Atwater once said, "Perception is reality." Psychologist Linda Humphreys said, "Perception molds, shapes, and influences our experience of our personal reality."[1] So when I'm vision-casting, I'm doing so through the lens of my reality.

My reality consists of two key components. First, my faith in God. I seek God's will in everything I do, including my vision. If God isn't part of my plans, then I'm wasting time. When God said His presence would not go with Moses and the Israelites, Moses said, "If your Presence does not go with us, do not send us up from here" (Exodus 33:15). Moses didn't want to move forward without God's presence in their midst, and that's how I live out my faith. I don't make plans and then ask if God wants to be part of my vision. I pray that God will reveal His plans and His vision for my life and that He will empower me to carry them out.

Second, my family. Everything I do, whatever is not reserved for God, is for them. I can't be present for work but not be present at home. I can't have a great vision as director chief but not have a vision for my family. I would be inconsistent if I put all my energy into my career and didn't include what happens at home. My family has been with me all along this journey, and they keep me grounded. I can't do any of what I do without them.

What is your vision, and how does it intersect with your reality? Vision is about the future, but it still must be grounded in the here and now. How do you share your vision with those you lead? Have you included the people in your personal life in your overall vision? How do you see yourself: as a bricklayer, a wall-builder, or a cathedral-builder?

Aligning the Vision

We may think that simply having a vision for our organization is enough.

It's not.

We may believe that having a vision and being passionate about it is enough to propel us and our organization to the next level.

It's not.

A critical component of leadership development is not just having a vision or being passionate about the vision you have, but knowing how to communicate, share, and align that vision and then know where you're going from there. What good is it to have a magnificent vision if it's not in sync with your organization or if it doesn't lead you anywhere? A vision that is not properly aligned with the mission of your organization will soon die, leaving goals unmet.

Being an effective leader means knowing when to step back from the vision and see where it needs alignment and adjustment to keep pace with the realities of your organization. Are you discerning enough to know when your vision is out of sync with the needs of those you lead, with local or national trends that may affect your organization? Are you sensitive enough to inner and outer elements that dictate a change in practices?

Not having an aligned vision can create chaos and confusion. Often, because the people we lead don't understand our direction, they may coalesce around competing factions within our organization, each one thinking they know and understand the vision when, in fact, no one does.

Perhaps the vision is fine, but your strategies to implement it are out of sync. But whether it's your vision or its alignment, fixing it is not just a one-time event. It's a continual process of work that leaders do on themselves and their vision. It's part of the much-needed development that we all must do to be effective and relevant.

An unaligned vision causes dissatisfaction and confusion. In some cases, it could be even more traumatic.

The fire department is all about saving lives. If my vision as fire chief is not aligned, it could have a ripple effect throughout the entire department and ultimately affect those we serve in the community.

Because we're in the business of saving lives, I feel the weight of the city on my shoulders. The direction of the fire department doesn't just stop with me. I don't want my vision to resonate because of my ego or because I'm trying to make a name for myself. I care about the future of the department because those persons under my leadership look to me to lead them, and the lives of people in our community are on the line.

That means I must think critically about where the department is headed and how we can get there while also paying attention to what's going on outside the department. It's difficult for us to navigate the organizational landscape or our communities' economic and civil uncertainties when our vision is in tatters. So it is crucial that we are vigilant with our vision and that we work to keep it relevant and firmly rooted in reality.

Clear Vision

Some of us have impaired vision. We visit optometrists to have our eyes checked, and we may leave with a prescription for glasses or contacts. If the problem is serious enough, we might need to visit an ophthalmologist who may recommend surgery. Those of us who have experienced impaired vision know how unpleasant it is not to be able to see things in the distance or read a book close up. How frustrating—and painful—it is to stumble into furniture while trying to get from one room to another, all because we can't see where we are going.

Now imagine a person trying to lead an organization without a clear vision. Leaders with no vision or with impaired vision will not be able to take the organization forward, meet expectations or goals, and achieve any progress if their vision is unclear and confusing. We have a responsibility not only to have a vision but to cast it clearly for those we lead. You're responsible for sharing a glimpse into the future of the organization, and then you build toward that future. Most people want future-focused leaders. Not many people want to work in an organization that is stuck in the past.

Having clarity gives others more confidence that we have a definite direction forward. When there is no clarity, those we lead feel insecure and worried, and their trust in our leadership will evaporate. None of our decisions and directives will make sense to them.

However, some people run into problems sharing and clarifying their vision with others. They miss valuable opportunities to engage with those they lead because they don't work to make sure the vision is clear for everyone. Instead, they retreat to their offices, send out directives, and delegate to other people the communication of the vision. In doing so, they abdicate their responsibility and create a leadership vacuum. This forces those they lead to go in different directions, depending on how they interpret the vision, causing chaos and confusion instead of unity and cohesion.

Habakkuk 2:2 says, "Write the vision, and make it plain." Effective leaders learn how to engage those they lead with vision by making the overall picture accessible. They also work with team members to strategize manageable steps to reach their goals. Then they can take those goals from mere ideas to vision and, ultimately, to reality.

Vision also needs context. Anything removed from its context loses meaning or can be misinterpreted, so you must provide proper context for your vision as you present it to your team. If they can't connect the dots and figure out how your vision is connected to the organization's overall goals, it will be hard to build much excitement around it. It won't be meaningful to anyone but you. Even if you have to revisit the context regularly, keep the vision and its meaning before your team so they can see what you see.

Visions die a quick death when we make a big splash in the beginning about the future but then push our plans to the backburner over time. If you seem bored after a few months, your team will be, too. I prefer to make the vision an integral part of our work every day. I am intentional about ensuring that the vision is interwoven into everything we do. I mention it frequently so my team knows I haven't forgotten our goals or allowed it to get stale.

We have to look ahead not just to the end of the week or the end of the month. Our plans are big-picture and are cast several years into the future. We must think long-term about how our decision will affect our organization past our tenure.

I know that as prepared as I am with plans that will further my vision, we will occasionally hit roadblocks. It's inevitable, but I'm not discouraged by the downturns. The best way to overcome this is to adapt, remain positive, and keep my team motivated as we get back on track.

Visionary Leadership

Having vision is all about figuring out your organization's "next." But there first must be a vision. If you're not always asking, "What's next for us?" perhaps you don't have a vision. Proverbs 29:18 says, "Where there is no vision, the people perish." Without a vision, an organization will be pulled in many different directions, get distracted, and not be as productive as it could be.

According to *Harvard Business Review,* "Visionary leadership does not just set the strategic direction—it tells a story about why the change is worth pursuing and inspires people to embrace the change."[2] I look for ways to engage my team because while I may have the big picture in mind, I need others to help me map out a strategy to get us there. Any feedback they give could be valuable in making the vision a reality, and I keep my mind ready to consider what they offer. I'm hoping that our work toward the vision will unify us and cultivate an environment of trust and open communication.

As a visionary, one of my goals is to talk less about myself and put more emphasis on our shared goals and vision. Some leaders miss what is most important. They are tempted to put themselves in the spotlight because of their position. They don't take advantage of the opportunity to unify their organization, their team, or their home because they make the vision all about themselves and leave others behind.

When I first became director chief, I tried to put my focus on those I would lead. I wanted to make sure they had the training and tools they needed and were respected in the community, and I wanted to cultivate a workplace that is progressive and inclusive.

When people think about the Nashville Fire Department or the Office of Emergency Management, I don't want them to think of me. I want the focus to be on those who work hard to keep the community safe and what we can offer Metro Nashville. I keep my decisions rooted in my core values, and they inform how I then find that delicate balance through visionary leadership—casting the vision but keeping the focus on the team and not just on myself.[3]

Shared Vision

Some of us take so much ownership of our vision that it's difficult for those we lead to get on board with us. We become siloed and think of ourselves as Lone Rangers who not only can cast our vision, but we can implement it, too. We have to ask ourselves, *Is my vision accessible to everyone, or am I guarding it closely so I alone can animate it? If I'm keeping my vision away from everyone else, why? Do I want all the credit, or do I believe that the only way it can get done is that I do it all myself?*

In the fire department, I can't do everything by myself. I need every person on my team to contribute to making the department what it is. That's why I strongly believe in a vision that can be shared so that we can unify around common goals and outcomes. That's the only way the department can be productive and thrive, and that's the only way our department can provide quality service to the residents of Nashville.

You need buy-in. You need people to be fully invested and unified around your vision. No one wants to feel that his or her contributions to the organization are being ignored so the leadership team can get all the credit. So the more you can bring people together around a definitive direction, the more valued and heard they will feel and the harder they will work to meet the organization's goals.

Vision adds meaning and direction to your shared work. It also keeps you connected to your organization and your team. You can usually spot leaders who don't have an organizational vision or who have not made it accessible. They take on a top position, build their brand, network for their next high-paying job, and then move on, often leaving the organization depleted, rudderless, and demoralized. They took advantage of an opportunity to promote themselves instead of helping and valuing their team or the organization. Even those with the best intentions simply can't lead without a vision, more specifically, without a shared vision.

As you share your vision and make it more accessible, you will see how impactful that decision will be. You will have created a community around your vision that will motivate and inspire others to move together in the same direction. Then you can tap into the excitement and energy in your organization for this common purpose and meaning.

Becoming a Visionary

When we visit an optometrist, he or she performs vision tests and eye exams, checks for abnormalities, and recommends adjustments for our glasses or contacts if needed. As leaders, we also need to take time to examine our vision and direction so that we can look for any problems in casting and communication and make the appropriate adjustments. When we go too long without regularly testing our vision and how we're imparting and implementing it, we may overlook problems that could easily be fixed and prevent further damage to our organizations.

For some of us, casting a vision, getting buy-in from our team members, figuring out how to collaborate, and keeping the vision fresh and out front can seem like a tall order. On top of that, add having to navigate any roadblocks along the way, and many of us will become frustrated before we reach our goals. Much of the initial action starts with you, so you'll need to rethink how you currently approach vision work. Organizational leadership expert Tony Robbins suggests leaders take the following steps:[4]

- **Take time for self-reflection.** "To determine vision, you must get in touch with your inner purpose—your ultimate reason for doing what you do every day." How many people engage in self-reflection when there's so much to do? If you're used to filling your days with a lot of distractions and noise, you may struggle with this activity at first. But keep working at it. Carve out time in your day to think about the "what" and the "why" of your vision. Once you've discovered that, then you can work with your team on the "how."

- **Be mindful.** "Practicing mindfulness can deepen your self-reflection and allow you to gain new insights that contribute to your leadership vision." This is another activity that asks you to look inward before casting outward. This activity might take practice, but when you're well-prepared to take on your vision, you can better prepare your team to join you.

- **Be positive.** Positivity seems to find its way in every aspect of leadership, but that's intentional. We need to be reminded to be optimistic and to help others to be optimistic, too. We want to practice positivity until it's ingrained in us, until it becomes as natural to us as breathing. Don't think you have to fake being positive. You should always be realistic. But even when circumstances aren't going the way you had planned, you can dig a bit deeper and find something to be grateful for and "identify your problems but give your power and energy to solutions."

- **Give clarity.** A vision that isn't clear isn't inspiring for anyone. "Today's employees seek meaningful work that will help them find fulfillment and feel like they're making a difference. . . . Leadership vision that does that will make them want to stick around." For the future of my team, I want to make sure the vision is clear for everyone. If not, then I've not been inclusive. I've left behind those who "don't get it." So, it's important for you to regularly revisit what you're asking your team to do.

- **Communicate.** "What is vision in leadership if you're not able to communicate it effectively?" Effective communication may look different for different members of your team. Communication is not a one-size-fits-all deal. To be effective, I may have one overall message that most people will hear and understand, but everyone's perception is different. If I'm paying attention, I know that I will also need to speak one-on-one with some of my team members because they may have more questions or want to clarify what I've said. And I might have to find other creative ways to engage people over time to make sure the message is conveyed effectively to everyone.

- **Take action.** Although your outward actions signal that you're ready to move forward, it's the work that came before, the preparations you've made, that will give you what you need to achieve your goals. You'll have confidence, and your team will be ready to help you.

Vision gives an organization focus, direction, meaning, and purpose. If we don't cast vision and provide much-needed direction, we are creating an atmosphere that will be chaotic and rudderless. Team members rely on us to communicate our vision and articulate the goals they will be expected to meet to fulfill that vision.

I want to give those I lead a glimpse into a productive and successful future so they will dream big and aspire to be "cathedral builders." I want to help them to develop a growth mindset that matches the vision I have for the department. If I don't lead with vision, I'm invalidating the purpose and meaning that my team members derive from their work.

I encourage all leaders to have a cohesive vision that delineates the direction they want their organization to go. If there's no clear vision, then work to develop one. Reach out to honest and supportive people who can come alongside you and provide resources that can help you draft a vision or deconstruct and repair your current vision. Having a vision for the future will provide long-term benefits for your organization, for those you lead and serve, and for you.

> *"A leader's job is to look into the future and see the organization, not as it is, but as it should be."*
> *Jack Welch*

Chapter Five

Communication

My wife and I have two sons, ages 15 and 27, and a grandson, who is six. When I talk to my family, I have to keep in mind that I'm talking to four different people who are at completely different places in their lives. I don't talk to my wife in the same way I talk to my six-year-old grandson. And there's a 12-year difference between my two sons, so each of them will have different perspectives and understandings about what I have to say. What I say may be important, but how I say it is just as important, too.

We lead people who are at different phases and stages. They come from different walks of life and have varied perspectives. It can become frustrating to try to customize your message for different people, but it's crucial to be flexible and adjust so that you can be effective.

It may be cliché, but communication is a two-way street. It doesn't just descend from the top down. I'm confident in who I am and the authority that I have, but I'm not too far up the ladder to turn away feedback and constructive criticism from those I lead. I invite their honesty and appreciate their sincerity. I know that they only want what's best for me and our organization.

Can You Hear Me Now?

Many of us may remember the cellphone commercial where the guy kept asking, "Can you hear me now?" When we run into difficulties communicating with those we lead, we may get extremely frustrated and want to repeatedly ask, "Can you hear me now? How about now?"

To take our organizations in a positive direction, we must hone our communication skills. Effective leaders understand that to inspire confidence and trust from those we lead and to take our organization higher, we must communicate in a way that will be understood by people at different phases and stages. We have to clear up any misunderstandings so that we can continue to move forward.

Some people may think that communication is only what they say in a team meeting or what they write in a memo or an email. But there are more ways to convey a message. We often overlook our body language, facial expressions, tone, and actions. And because we forget that we're communicating in these silent but important ways, we may present conflicting messages to those we lead. We expect them to read our minds or interpret what we mean, but that opens up more opportunities to misunderstand what we're trying to say.

I try to be aware of how I can get my message across. I don't want to be misunderstood or offend someone without realizing it. I also strategize how I communicate. I concentrate on two main areas: listening and self-reflection. Notice that I didn't mention talking. There's a time for me to talk, but if I want to improve communication, I have to be willing to be present so others can express themselves, too.

When I'm actively listening (not just hearing), I can see how effective my message is. I'm checking to see if the person I'm listening to has clarity and understanding. If it seems that we're not aligned, then that tells me something has gone wrong. It provides me with a real-time opportunity to correct or adjust my communication strategies. Listening challenges me. It allows me to make myself more accessible and to receive what others have to say. Active listening is just as crucial to how leaders communicate as it is to what they say because it forces us to be accountable for what we're hearing.

I've tried to discipline myself in listening through prayer. I don't want to enter into prayer with God and do all the talking. Although He patiently listens to all my petitions, I also need to leave room for Him to speak and for me to listen. It's easier to just start talking until we've said what's on our minds. It's much more difficult for us to listen with open ears and open hearts.

Self-reflection gives me time to assess how I communicate. I often replay conversations in my mind and think, *Did I say that the right way? Should I have said it differently? How effective was I in getting my message across?* The key to an accurate assessment is to be honest without being overly critical. But more importantly, I need to use the information I gather to make the necessary changes.

Leaders usually control the narrative in our organizations. It's our responsibility to keep everyone informed with facts, not office gossip. I send out a video message to my team every quarter. I talk about what's happening, good and bad. I want to make sure that they hear from me so they don't have to wonder about rumors floating around. I want to maintain their trust in me and keep us unified and on track.

Mindful Leadership

Many of the people we lead view leadership as inaccessible hierarchies that hand down edicts and assignments that they then must follow. They don't feel valued and heard; instead, they feel treated as just another cog in the machine. They see a wide gap between their leadership team and the rest of the people in the organization. Why is that?

We often make the mistake of building walls around our positions, closing ourselves off from our team. There have been attempts by leaders to give people access. For example, many organizations have implemented an "open-door policy" where any employee can feel comfortable meeting with leadership and discussing what's on their minds.

While an open-door policy is a start by creating an environment of trust and beginning the conversation, I don't believe that it goes far enough. Simply telling team members we will meet with them and listen to their suggestions, concerns, or complaints won't provide effective solutions if we aren't willing to be transparent and empathetic.

The reason transparency and empathy are missing from our communication is that leaders make this policy as one-sided as possible. Employees can meet with us and talk about what they're thinking, but we may not reciprocate. We believe it's okay for them to be transparent, but when was the last time we were transparent with those we lead? Have we shared our heart and passion with our teams? How empathetic are we? Do we have the capacity to be sensitive to others and their different experiences?

Most of us would like to believe that we are transparent to some degree and that we are compassionate and caring. But we know that to demonstrate those characteristics, we must first be vulnerable, and that's not a place most leaders want to find themselves. To be vulnerable is to appear weak, to be powerless.

We often avoid the personal aspects of leadership because engaging with those we lead at that level will expose us in a way we may not want to be exposed to. So we build walls and siloes around ourselves that may allow for one-way vulnerability on the part of those in our organizations but not reciprocal vulnerability from us.

Leadership teams also make the mistake of substituting micromanaging tactics that foster an environment of distrust and suspicion. We assume because we are getting things done that we are good communicators, everyone understands us, and they are on board with the direction we're going. But when we are intentional about engaging with those we lead, being present and compassionate, we find that we don't have to have needless boundaries or micromanage every aspect of every assignment. Instead, we build trust with our team members, who then are more eager to participate with us in shared goals.

When we're not mindful of the experiences and voices of our team, or we're not willing to engage and be transparent, our communication grows stagnant and works against the vision and community we're trying to build. And when we build walls and hide behind our position in the organizational hierarchy, we can't form more authentic relationships with those we lead.

Effective communication is compromised and makes it more difficult for us to build trust. If those we lead believe we're distant and not authentic, they won't be open either. Despite our paying lip service to open-door conversations, team members already know they're not having an honest and open exchange with us.

People can sense when we lack the compassion to understand their experiences and perspectives. Leaders may be so absorbed with results or their own career path that they don't fully appreciate or care about what others may be saying. But when we put our egos aside and listen intently, we can earn trust and build comradery.

Ultimately, being a mindful leader who is willing to listen and share our experiences leads to greater accountability and strengthens us to take positive action. Team members won't trust us if we hear what they say but take no action. We have a responsibility not just to listen and talk but to take seriously the conversations we have and see how best they can spur us to make the necessary changes. When we work to be mindful in these areas, we can become much better and more effective communicators.

Becoming a Better Communicator

I've often been inspired by the words of great orators, such as Dr. Martin Luther King Jr. His speech "I Have a Dream" is part of the soundtrack of the Civil Rights Movement. There's no doubt that King was a great communicator. His words brought people together as they marched for freedom.

But some of us struggle to communicate effectively. When God called Moses to lead the children of Israel, Moses said, "I have never been eloquent, neither in the past nor even now that you have spoken to your servant, but I am slow of speech and slow of tongue" (Exodus 4:10). Moses was tasked with leading several million people out of slavery in Egypt, but he told God he didn't have the skills to speak to them. He knew he wouldn't be effective if he couldn't communicate.

God promised to be with Moses and to send Aaron, Moses' brother, to support him. Many scholars have debated what Moses meant when he said he was "slow of speech and slow of tongue." Perhaps he had a speech impediment or some other speech delay. What we do know is that Moses' ability to communicate was so important that God promised to help him overcome his hesitancy.

There are many organizational leadership experts and trainers who offer advice on how we can communicate more effectively. If we can't convey our message and clearly articulate our vision, our organization will suffer. According to *Forbes* magazine, there are several ways we can improve our communication skills.[1]

- **Always speak honestly.** You can be the most skilled speaker, but if people think that what you say is dishonest, exaggerated, or lacking integrity, they will stop listening. Trust, once lost, is hard to regain. Be honest. I want to create a track record that people can trust, and I find that the people I lead are more open and honest with me because they know I've been honest with them.

- **Get personal.** "Stop issuing corporate communications and begin having organizational conversations—think dialogue, not monologue." People appreciate when leaders see them and hear them as individuals and not just as replaceable employees. Being intentional about having one-on-one conversations with your team can go a long way in making you more relatable and accessible. Don't be aloof or keep yourself at arm's length. My team's feedback is crucial to my success and the success of our organization, but I won't be able to hear that feedback or learn from it if I don't cultivate relationships where people feel comfortable talking to me about what's on their minds.

- **Be specific.** Communicate with clarity. "Simple and concise is always better than complicated and confusing." Get to the point of what you're saying quickly, and don't spend too much time on preliminaries. "Make your words count." You don't want people to tune you out before you can convey your message. Once you've set the example for specificity, you can expect the same from your team.

- **Focus on what you give and not so much on what you receive.** "The key is to approach each interaction with a servant's heart." Focus on what your team needs and wants instead of what you can get out of the interaction. We sometimes forget that it isn't all about us. But if we want to keep learning and growing, we have to be other-focused instead of always being self-focused.

- **Replace ego with empathy.** "Empathetic communicators display a level of authenticity and transparency that is not present with those who choose to communicate behind the carefully crafted façade propped up by a very fragile ego." You can transform relationships by putting your ego aside and showing your concern and care for your team. Don't allow your position to put a wedge between you and those you lead. You need your team, and they need you because neither can go it alone.

- **Read between the lines.** Sometimes it's more about what's not said than what is said. Since there are several ways people communicate and express themselves, develop the skill of listening to more than just their words. Be alert to facial expressions, body language, and tone. Don't be so quick to fill the space with words. "Keep your eyes and ears open and your mouth shut, and you'll be amazed at how your level of organizational awareness is raised."

- **Know what you're talking about.** Make sure you have a mastery of your subject matter when you speak. "Most successful people have little interest in listening to those individuals who cannot add value to a situation or topic." Leaders shouldn't talk simply because they love the sound of their own voices. If your team members perceive that you're not credible, they won't listen.

Most of us understand that we need to communicate with others, but a flurry of emails or directives handed down in a meeting is not the only, nor the most effective, way to engage with those on our team. Great leaders must seek meaningful ways to convey their vision but also to make communication an authentic, reciprocal conversation.

We can start by asking ourselves how mindful we are. *How transparent are we willing to be with those we lead?*

Can we sit in a vulnerable space and have a dialogue with team members so that we can foster an environment of trust for everyone?

Many leaders may be tempted to skip this crucial part of self-examination and jump right into trying to promote their vision. But buy-in from team members usually comes when they feel safe and know they can trust the leadership team and the direction they're going. That's difficult to do when we aren't accessible, transparent, and empathetic.

But once we have established trust, then we can focus on relaying information to move the company forward as we work to keep our message clear and precise. The vehicle for keeping people excited and engaged with our vision and the plans to get there is good communication.

*"You can have brilliant ideas,
but if you can't get them across,
your ideas won't get you anywhere."*
Lee Iacocca

Chapter Six

Servanthood

Coming to know Christ is the decision of a lifetime. Fortunately, my journey started early. I was introduced to God as a child, and my parents taught me the importance of faith. Dad was a deacon at church, and he spent his life serving other people. He understood that our lives on earth are short, so we should focus on our relationship with Christ and His promise of eternal life. I learned from my parents and other people in the community that serving God and helping those in need should always be our focus. They taught me to have a servant's heart and not to be self-centered.

I've gained so much from Jesus' teachings. I strive to walk in humility, build up and strengthen my faith, seek God for guidance, and keep Him at the center of my life. Not only does this give me great comfort and reassurance, but the Holy Spirit also keeps me attuned to the needs of others. As part of my life's work, I aim to help and support as many people as I can in my family, my church, and my community.

One year, Metro Nashville's government was experiencing a tight budget crunch. This meant most government employees would not be receiving cost-of-living-adjustment raises or step (within grade) raises that year. As a department head, however, I was eligible for a raise; but I thought about my team and how they would have to face a year without extra money in their pockets to take care of their families.

I don't tell this to brag on myself or to boost my ego. I have compassion for my team, and it's my responsibility to address their needs. I couldn't ignore the fact that my team was not going to get their well-deserved raises, so I was compelled to do something about it.

Instead of taking my raise, I distributed my extra earnings among my team. I intended to do this discreetly, but word got around, and it was leaked to the press. Before long, the whole city knew of my generosity. Another department head said, "That's what a true leader would do!" I was humbled by the comments from my colleagues, but that wasn't why I did it. I simply wanted my team members to know I cared about them and wanted to reward them for their hard work.

I've always believed that if you want to know who a person is, give that person power and watch how he or she will use it. Being a servant leader is difficult at times. I must use restraint and discipline to lead and make decisions without letting my emotions overwhelm me. But I work to achieve that balance so that I can be focused on the needs of others.

What Is a Servant Leader?

The concept of *servant leadership* has been around for a long time, but the phrase has been overused and has somewhat lost its true meaning. Every leader isn't a servant leader, and that may be appropriate depending on the organization. But for some people, becoming servant leaders is a radical departure from what they usually experience in corporate culture. As servant leaders, they are more interested in bringing about unity, empowerment, and trust to their organizations than in wielding power and making a name for themselves.

Servant leaders differ from the traditional "command-and-control leaders" because they are more focused on meeting the needs of their team. This is the type of culture I want in my organization. I'm not the boss who instills fear in those I lead, and I'm not interested in just having power over others.

As chief, I have authority, but I'm also other-focused. I don't seek the spotlight for myself or put myself on a pedestal. Instead, I want to promote other people. I want to help them develop confidence and the skills they need to be successful. Engaging the collective to work and solve problems is how I would like for the team to thrive.

I've had to develop good listening skills as I've worked to become an active listener. I have empathy for those I lead. It's hard to connect with my team and make decisions that are in their best interest if I can't put myself in their place and understand how they might feel. Being aware is another aspect of my leadership. I have to be tuned in to what's going on around me and develop strategies that will effectively mitigate problems and crises.

As a servant leader, I can't be overly sensitive or easily offended. I may be in charge, but I'm confident enough to take criticism and feedback. I can hear from team members and not punish them for having diverse ideas or when they disagree with me. I have to be selfless, put others first, and encourage others to succeed.

Turning the Hierarchy on Its Head

As Jesus said, "The last will be first, and the first will be last." In Jesus' day, this was a radical statement. There were highly respected leaders who relished their vaunted positions over those on the margins, those who had little if any influence. But Jesus' statement sums up the life of servanthood even today. This mindset turns corporate hierarchy on its head and causes us to look more deeply at how we engage with those we lead.

We may be accustomed to having an entourage, a group of people who are there to serve us, cater to our wishes, and handle the toughest and most menial tasks so we don't have to. They make it easier for us to navigate life and focus on the things we think are most important. Unfortunately, some of us take for granted those persons we believe are below us. We lose the ability to see their needs or listen to their concerns. Over time, they become almost invisible to us unless we need them for something.

But what if we took a different approach? What if we led with humility and put those we lead in the spotlight? What if we stopped expecting to be waited on or moved away from a self-focused leadership model that has leaders at the center and instead decided to serve others? That's what it means to be a servant leader.

Some of us may be afraid to model servanthood in what can feel like a cutthroat corporate atmosphere. It's a climate that encourages people to look out for themselves and no one else or risk losing whatever power they may have. We may feel intimidated by going against the hierarchal model.

We have to do the internal work to be effective servant leaders. If we are insecure, it will be even more difficult to put others out front and be other-focused. It may seem counterintuitive, but the stronger you are, the easier it is to serve. It's the weak and insecure leaders who struggle with serving others with humility and care. They wonder, *What if my efforts to put others out front backfire on me or is not in the best interest of the organization?*

However, many experts say that the benefits of servant leadership are a win for everyone involved. You will learn what it means to authentically communicate, engage, connect, and be in partnership with your team members. You can then more dynamically help other people realize their purpose and potential.

The Perfect Servant Leader

I've been blessed to have many different people in my life who have served as great examples of leadership, but I've had no better model than Jesus Christ. This makes perfect sense because as a Christian with a biblical worldview, I see Him as the perfect example of having total authority but the humility to make Himself accessible to humanity.

When I think of Jesus' servant leadership, I'm reminded of the passage of Scripture in John 13:4-5 that describes the events leading up to His crucifixion. Jesus and His disciples had just finished the Last Supper, and now Jesus did something extraordinary.

> [Jesus] got up from supper, took off his outer robe, and tied a towel around himself. Then he poured water into a basin and began to wash the disciples' feet and to wipe them with the towel that was tied around him.

Jesus, the Son of God, washed the feet of His disciples! To understand just how amazing this act of humility is, you'd have to understand ancient Near East culture. People walked virtually everywhere, and their feet were dirty when they arrived at their destination. A host would offer guests hospitality by making sure the guests' feet were washed, but usually, that was the job of servants.

By washing His disciples' feet, Jesus was showing humility and modeling servant leadership for them. He was no less powerful by taking on the role of a servant. But before His death, He was leaving for them a legacy of humility, having a servant's heart, and putting others' needs before their own. They would need this after Jesus left them. Then Jesus revealed His reason for washing their feet (John 13:6-9):

> He came to Simon Peter, who said to him,
> "Lord, are you going to wash my feet?" Jesus
> answered, "You do not know now what
> I am doing, but later you will understand."
> Peter said to him, "You will never wash my
> feet." Jesus answered, "Unless I wash you,
> you have no share with me." Simon Peter
> said to him, "Lord, not my feet only but also
> my hands and my head!"

Being a Christian means being like Christ, and the only hierarchy I care about is where Jesus is first, others are second, and I am third. I live my life so I can follow Jesus' example because I want to be as much like Him as I can. I look for opportunities to be more like Jesus. That's why I spend time in prayer and in reading the Bible. This is what sustains me and helps me to be more compassionate.

What Is Your Leadership Style?

Servant leadership is just one of many styles of leadership. I think every person should incorporate some component of servanthood, but how much will depend on the organizational environment. But in thinking about servant leadership, I want to inspire you to be the best you can be, which might mean you incorporate elements of various styles to be more effective. The following information could help you figure out your style (or styles) of leadership.[1]

- *Coaches* are motivational.
- *Visionaries* are progress-focused and inspirational.
- *Servant leaders* are humble and protective.
- *Autocratic leaders* are authoritarian and result-focused.
- *Laissez-faire, or hands-off, leaders* are autocratic and delegatory.
- *Democratic leaders* are supportive and innovative.
- *Pacesetters* are helpful and motivational.
- *Transformational leaders* are always challenging and communicative.
- *Transactional leaders* are performance-focused.
- *Bureaucratic leaders* are hierarchical and duty-focused.

Think about how you currently lead. What styles best describe your leadership? Now think about how you would like to lead. What styles best describe you in the future?

Becoming a Servant Leader

I don't lead as a servant because I want to brag about what I'm doing. I just want the best for other people. I care about them, and I want every decision I make to be in their best interest so that we all can succeed. I want to inspire as many people as I can to rethink their leadership style and consider being servant leaders or at least incorporate some of the key components of servanthood into their leadership.

How can you develop a servant's heart? How can you be a better servant leader? Consider the following steps to develop your leadership skills:[2]

- **Lead by example.** "As a servant leader, you should be willing to do anything that you ask your team to do." Your team members want to know that you will put in just as much work as they do, which will motivate them and gain their trust.

- **Show people why their job is important.** "When employees feel that what they do is important to the overall success of the organization, they usually feel more empowered and are willing to work harder to help it succeed." Your team wants to know that what they're doing is meaningful and connected to a much bigger purpose. It's your job as a servant leader to help them connect the dots and understand the "why" of what they're doing.

- **Let them know that they are heard and seen.** When employees feel like just another cog in the wheel, they feel that they don't matter. If you are a person who treats your team members as if they are replaceable and indistinguishable from anyone else who could fill their seats, then your team probably doesn't have high morale. Instead, let your team know that their voices and opinions matter and that you listen to them and value their work and their feedback.

- **Be your team's biggest cheerleader.** Don't hog the spotlight. As a servant leader, be more "interested in helping [your] team members become great leaders." Become invested in their development and success. Encourage them to further their education or participate in programs that will help them to grow. Encourage them to achieve the proper work/life balance. Instead of promoting yourself, promote your team, and inspire them to shine.

Many of us don't mind volunteering our time to help people in need and participating in other charitable giving. But that's where many of us stop in our willingness to serve others. We may not have considered making servanthood part of our corporate identity as well.

It can take a lot of courage to become a servant leader. It's a radical departure from the hierarchical model so many organizations have adopted, and it means relinquishing control of the lives and potential of the people on our team. Not only do many of us fear pushback from our organization for making servanthood part of our identity, but some of us are not secure enough to put power and ambition aside to lead with humility.

Servanthood means approaching leadership with a mixture of humility, compassion, empathy, and integrity. If we view our responsibility as akin to stewardship instead of ownership, it may make it easier for some of us to shift our focus to serving others. When we acknowledge that part of our responsibility is to help others realize their potential instead of holding them back for our own agenda, we can better understand our role as servant leaders.

I look to Jesus as my example of servant leadership. I don't worry about compromising my position when I focus on team members and engage with them in a way that encourages and serves them. I know that by putting others first, the fire department and the people of Nashville reap the benefits.

"The first and most important choice a leader makes
is the choice to serve, without which one's capacity
to lead is severely limited."
Robert Greenleaf

Chapter Seven

Responsibility

As chief of the Nashville Fire Department, the buck stops with me. Instead of looking for someone to blame, I must deal with conflicts, misunderstandings, disagreements, bruised egos, and miscommunication. Shakespeare is often credited with saying, "Heavy is the head that wears the crown."

It's difficult to be the one who has the responsibility of sorting out various problems. I must be able to read and assess situations and bring a sense of calm and understanding into the environment. If I've done my job effectively, everyone will be satisfied, but that's not always the case.

I've been in situations where I shouldered blame that wasn't mine. But I believe in solving problems, not pushing them off on someone else. Responsible people step up and look for ways to work through problems. Whether we are the coach of a Little League team, own a business, lead a ministry group at church, or raise our children, those we lead are looking to us to be accountable to work through the problems and make responsible decisions that affect them. In the absence of responsible leadership, there is chaos, and no one feels safe.

A few years ago, I attended a fire department graduation ceremony that seemed to be going well at first. But then we ran into difficulties with our master of ceremony. Several days later, I went to the mayor's office to answer for what had happened.

Although the persons in charge had signed off on the order of the program at the graduation, and I wasn't responsible for what the MC said at the ceremony, I knew that as chief, I couldn't point fingers at other people and hide behind what others might have done. Instead, I assured the mayor that I didn't know what had gone wrong, but I would take responsibility, get to the bottom of it, and make sure that it wouldn't happen again on my watch. I believe that's what I should have done as an effective leader.

When I got back to my department, I had two tasks: First, find out what happened. Second, move on. When I'm in meetings and we're discussing something that happened, I don't let my team get too bogged down in the minutiae of the problem. It's appropriate to discuss it, but we can't waste time wallowing in shame and blame. At some point, we have to fix the problem and then ask, "What's next?" As a responsible leader, it's my job to keep us on track and not allow us to be distracted by what happened.

Excuses, Excuses

George Washington Carver said, "Ninety-nine percent of all failures come from people who have a habit of making excuses." People make excuses so they won't have to be accountable or responsible for what has happened. They may play the victim so they won't have to answer for their actions. And if they never take responsibility, they also never make much progress in fixing the problems. They have to first own problematic situations and then seek the best strategies to solve the problems.

We can't make excuses for ourselves or create an atmosphere where team members feel comfortable making excuses. I know that taking responsibility is part of my job. Knowing this doesn't make it any easier, but I understand that my success rests on my ability to take responsibility not only for my actions but for my behavior and my attitude.

How we handle tasks can make or break the trust others have placed in us. If we take on responsibility but do so with a bad attitude or while complaining to others about what we have to do, that's just as problematic as shirking responsibility. We need people who trust us to see that we are mature enough to meet our challenges head-on with a positive attitude that reflects our overall vision for the organization.

When I was talking with the mayor about what happened at the graduation ceremony, that was a low moment for me. We had worked hard to make that ceremony special for the graduates and the guests, but it wasn't the success we had hoped for. In a rush to avoid fault, I could have given him a list of other people to blame, but I didn't because that's not why I became the chief. I don't want excuses, finger-pointing, and victimhood to be my legacy. Instead, I want to be proactive and accountable for what happens under my leadership.

When people remember me long after I've left this position, I want them to remember Chief William Swann as a man of integrity and a fair, honorable, and responsible person. I also want them to see me as someone who leads by example even when it's not easy to do so. This is the part of leadership that isn't always pleasant, but effective leaders don't shy away from it because it's unpleasant. I don't demand of others what I don't demand first of myself, and this is the blueprint when I model responsibility.

Excuses are obstacles and make us weak. They hinder an organization's productivity and progress and contribute to distrust, confusion, anger, and uncertainty among team members. I don't know of anyone who got ahead because he or she relied on excuses, but I know many people who have excelled because they refused to offer excuses. Instead, they took responsibility and earned the respect of those they lead.

Benjamin Franklin said, "He that is good for making excuses is seldom good for anything else." Not accepting responsibility is a form of dishonesty, and once we get a reputation for not being honest, we lose our influence and trust. What good are we then to our organization?

Our team members notice when we pass the buck and put other people in the line of fire. They may believe that someday they'll be the ones who get blamed, so they can't trust us to be responsible and trustworthy. Real leadership means stepping up and being honest, not trying to paper over our mistakes or flaws by blaming others.

Responsibility is integral to what we do, so we can't easily set it aside or ignore it. It is so essential that I'm not sure a person can lead without it. If you remove responsibility from the equation, what's left that sets a leader apart? We must be willing to say that the buck stops with us and that we are strong enough to take on whatever comes our way. If we're not ready to take responsibility, we're not ready to lead. And if we're not ready to lead, we have some work to do.

Step Up

The reason many of us struggle with taking responsibility is that we're not positioned to do so. The ability to handle the obligations of leadership doesn't just happen. For most people, it's a skill that has to be acquired and then honed. But first, a person must be self-aware enough to realize that he or she needs to work on that skill. Unfortunately, many leaders seem oblivious to how poorly they handle responsibility.

If you have put your team at arm's length and you lead your organization through emails, it's difficult to know what's going on, especially when things go wrong. You need to stay informed about what's going on with your team members. This means you need to keep all lines of communication open and be ready to use a hands-on approach so that as problems arise, you know what's going on and can step up.

Then offer leadership resources and a strong network of support, but don't wait until problems arise. Be supportive all the time, and give team members what they need to solve problems before those problems get out of hand.

Depending on the size and scope of an organization, it's appropriate to delegate responsibility. But I don't want to be so eager to push tasks off on others if I know it will cause problems for them and the department. Perhaps they're not ready for those tasks, or maybe taking on more assignments will cause their regular workload to suffer. If I need to offer more training or support before I involve team members, then that becomes part of how I make sure they can take ownership.

Not only do we have to handle occupational mistakes and the issues surrounding them, but we may also find ourselves confronted with internal injustices and competing ideologies. How do we deal with issues that are so personal and that may not be directly associated with the organization? Some of those we lead or those who work alongside us bring their personal biases to work with them.

At times, we have to play referee and bring calm and a sense of unity. Sometimes we must remind people of basic common decency and their responsibility to be professional and to leave the hot-button issues at home. It's not our job to take sides or cause more division. Our first organizational allegiance is to help us to unify as a team and find as much common ground as possible. Our success and productivity depend on it. It's up to us to be agents for positive change and make a difference in our organizations.

Transformative leadership occurs when I show the fire department that I'm not hiding behind my position and shifting blame to others so I won't look bad. Instead, I've worked hard to establish a healthy ecosystem where I model responsibility, and I also facilitate an environment where everyone is encouraged to seek solutions. In that environment, I want to mitigate any chaos and confusion that occurs when things don't go to plan so that everyone feels valued and not blamed. It is a place where we can speak honestly to one another even if that includes offering constructive criticism.

Being responsible also means being able to receive criticism without becoming angry or bitter. This is where a positive attitude and follow-up behavior carry me forward. I have to listen intently to what critics are saying and learn from it.

While we may not like to be told we have made a mistake or that others are displeased with what we've done, it could be a gold mine of information for us. We should discover what we can learn from it and then see how we can fix what's wrong. Every criticism is not a personal attack, and if we remain open-minded, we can use the criticism to explore new avenues to be productive and successful.

Criticism of any kind is hard to hear, but good leaders know that being overly sensitive limits our ability to be accountable. Remember that what we do is not just about us. We may be the face of our unit, department, or organization, but what we do is for our team and those we serve. As fire chief, I have an obligation to those who work for the fire department, but I also have a responsibility to those we serve in the community.

Becoming a Responsible Leader

For years, I've worked to cultivate an environment of honesty and trust in my organization. I want my colleagues and those I lead to know that we will be accountable and take responsibility for problems, but we will also always focus on solutions more than we will focus on the problems. And we will always ask, "What's next?" so that we can move forward and lean into our future rather than continually rehashing the problems of the past.

Being responsible is a characteristic that some leaders struggle with. They prefer taking the easy way out and offering up a variety of excuses to take the heat off themselves, which is not the way to excel. If you want to be more responsible, consider these suggestions:[1]

- **When you're faced with problems or blamed for something that went wrong, don't lash out or find other people to blame.** You might not be the one who messed up, but as the leader, you can figure out the "who," "how," and "why" later. First, mitigate the situation as best you can. Then think through how you can unify your team and discuss and process what happened in a way that is helpful to all.

- **Make informed ethical judgments about existing norms and policies.** You might have to take responsibility for something that happened, but you also have to carefully consider if a breach of conduct deserves disciplinary action or more careful supervisory strategies. Hopefully, it doesn't come to this point, but if it does, be prepared.

- **Display moral courage and aspire to positive change.** The people you lead need to see you as a courageous leader who can lead them past the crisis and make changes in the future so it won't happen again. Your positive actions will inspire their confidence in you to be a problem-solver and someone who has their best interest at heart.

- **Engage in long-term thinking and in gaining a realistic perspective.** It's difficult to see everything during a crisis. Sometimes it's not until it's over and the problems are solved that we can get a better perspective on what happened. What you learned as you were handling the problem will be valuable for you in the future. Incorporate what you learned in your long-term planning and vision. It will give you a better perspective and help you when you face similar situations.

- **Encourage collective problem-solving.** Leaders should have broad shoulders upon which we can carry a lot of responsibility, but we still don't have to solve all our organization's problems alone. Instead, we should encourage our team to come together to offer solutions and be invested and engaged in the outcomes. Collectively, we can be more creative and expansive in how we handle problems because we have a variety of perspectives that give us unique insight. Leverage the collective to bring a greater depth of support and better solutions to the table.

Jesus' teachings inspire me, especially when it comes to being a responsible leader. Jesus taught His disciples,

"From everyone to whom much has been given, much will be required, and from the one to whom much has been entrusted, even more will be demanded" (Luke 12:48).

We have many tasks placed on our shoulders, so we're expected to step up and be accountable for what we need to do. That's not unreasonable; it's simply what goes with the territory. Those responsibilities come with the title, and we're obligated to deal with them. But where we excel is when we willingly become accountable by owning them and doing our best to deal with them in a way that honors our organization, our team members, and ourselves.

Our organizations won't grow and prosper when all we have to offer are excuses, rationalizations, and justifications. Irresponsible leaders don't grow. They jump from position to position, leaving disaster in their wake. Team members lose trust in leadership, and morale plummets. But we need to be strong enough to take on the tasks—and burdens—of leadership while moving everyone forward and making good long-term decisions.

Irresponsible leaders aren't sustainable. They can't instill trust, build community, and encourage buy-in around organizational vision. For most of us when we were growing up, it took time for us to develop a sense of responsibility. But as we got older and matured, we could be trusted to take on more and be depended on to do what we were asked to do.

To be responsible means making informed decisions that will have a short-term effect on us, but those decisions will also have a long-term effect on our organization that may outlast our careers. We need to be aware of internal issues as well as external trends and events.

All of these have an impact on our decisions and how we respond, so we have to become visionaries who are aware of the footprint our decisions will make now and into the future. We must make responsible decisions that will benefit and not harm others for years to come.

"The price of greatness is responsibility."
Winston Churchill

Chapter Eight

Learning

An effective leader can glean knowledge from anywhere. My "experiential knowledge" includes all the personal experiences that have taught me many life lessons. But I also can pick up "observational knowledge." That happens when I open myself to learning from the experiences of others.

Chief Ricky White shared a profound experience with me. I have included his story to demonstrate why we should be open to learning even from unexpected places!

"I was called out on a situation that involved a hazardous material truck. The driver tried to drive under a bridge that had a clearance of about 12 feet, but the truck was taller than that. So when the driver tried to go under the bridge, the truck got wedged under it. When I arrived on the scene, I assessed the situation. I realized that if we tried to free the truck, we might rupture the container, spilling hazardous material and posing a danger to everyone in the immediate area.

"We called in our hazmat team and representatives from the Tennessee Department of Transportation. We huddled together to try to figure out how to move this truck without putting anyone in danger, and the atmosphere was tense. We tried our best to come up with a solution, but despite all our expertise, we were stumped.

"Then, seemingly out of nowhere, a little boy rode his bike to the scene. He was about eight or nine years old. He ignored the perimeter we had set up and wasn't fazed by all the important fire and rescue officials standing around trying to figure out what to do.

" 'What's going on?' he asked.

" 'Hey, stay back!' we yelled, trying to shoo away the boy as we kept trying to solve the puzzle, but he stayed put. Hoping to hurry him away from the area, we finally explained the situation to him, telling him that we may have to evacuate the area because we didn't think we could successfully free the truck without rupturing the container. The boy looked at the truck and made his own assessment.

" 'Why don't you just let the air outta the tires?'

" 'What?' We couldn't believe that within minutes of arriving on the scene, this boy was offering a solution, especially one we hadn't thought of.

" 'Just let the air out of the tires.'

"Then the light bulb went on for me, and I realized that his suggestion just might work. I went over and told all the other uniformed bigwigs what the boy said without telling them where I got the idea. We let a little air out of the truck's tires, and though we couldn't move the truck forward, we were able to back it out without causing any damage to the container. After we had successfully cleared the truck, everyone congratulated me for coming up with the idea, but I pointed to the boy on the bike. I don't think they could have been any more surprised. They couldn't believe this young boy had solved the problem and no damage or contamination had occurred.

"I learned a life lesson that day. Sometimes we have tunnel vision. We're so deep in the weeds, we can't see what's in front of us. We can become so fixated on one single aspect that we miss other parts of the problem that may suggest the needed solution. That's why it's important to keep an open mind and not miss an opportunity to learn.

"I frequently tell this story because it illustrates a brilliant learning moment for me. I'm not ashamed to admit that a little boy on a bike taught me something that none of the adults could figure out."

Jesus instructs us to be patient with children and not to shun them. When Jesus was teaching, someone brought a group of children to Him, but His disciples tried to send them away. Jesus said, "Suffer the little children to come unto me, and forbid them not: for of such is the kingdom of God" (Mark 10:14). I believe this is an important warning not to overlook unlikely sources of help, no matter where they may come from.

Growth Mindset

The willingness to learn helps us develop a growth mindset, which is "the attitude and belief that we can all improve our skills, abilities, and emotional intelligence with time, effort, and energy." We can potentially learn from any experience, any person, at any time. Even our failures and mistakes can be fertile ground for growth, although it may not seem that way at the time. "The best leaders learn from experiences—including failures—and apply those lessons to unfamiliar situations in the future."[1]

When we have a growth mindset, we can drive innovation, build great teams, and make ourselves and those we lead more resilient.[2] We recognize the fact that learning takes place every day,[3] but if we miss out on life's lessons, we will be stagnant in our leadership. So, a conscientious leader will "make time for the hard work that continual learning requires."[4]

Effective leaders are intentional about making time to learn. Charles Brindamour, CEO of Intact in Canada, says when he first went to Intact, "he blocked out three to four hours every morning to gain a better understanding of areas that could influence his company or the lives of his employees. . . . 'If you don't make this a priority, you risk the organization becoming complacent.'"[5]

I never let my ego get in the way of learning. When I tell Chief White's story of the boy on the bike, that is my way of letting people know that you can learn the greatest lessons in the most unexpected places. I consider it a blessing that the Lord allows me to learn new things and gain more knowledge, no matter the source. I encourage you also to adopt a growth mindset that will open you to new possibilities and opportunities you might not have considered before.

Leadership Development

Most of the skills we need to be effective are taught. While some of those skills are intuitive and natural to some people, most of us have to learn those skills and figure out how to apply them effectively. Top-level leaders are the ones who always take advantage of opportunities to learn, whether it's in a classroom, on an interactive digital platform, or through peer-to-peer learning. There are multiple benefits to continuous education.

The need for leadership development is always high, and the leadership training industry is a billion-dollar industry. Executives, managers, and those who aspire to lead want to improve, and organizations will pay millions of dollars to train them. But industry experts don't agree that the traditional education route is the best way for good leaders to get the education they need.

Stagnant leaders cease to be a driving force in their organizations. Their vision may grow stale, they find it difficult to navigate the changing culture around them, and they don't understand the team members and communities they serve. But leaders who are always open to learning more and developing themselves find it much easier to grasp new concepts, recruit and mentor more people, and streamline their path to achieve their vision.

Transformative leaders take advantage of educational opportunities and encourage quality education for their team members. But traditional education isn't the only way for us to learn. Theory and classroom training are good, but they don't always offer learning that applies to the changing climate of our organizations. Also, they aren't always flexible enough to keep up with technology, busy schedules, or constantly changing global concerns.

The key for us to unlock our potential and stay open to learning opportunities is to embrace more efficient and accessible forms of education in addition to whatever traditional education we've already had. These include peer-to-peer learning and digital formats. We should share those same opportunities with our team members and others in the organization so that they can be better prepared for the needs that our work may require.

Most people want to work smarter, not harder, and that won't look like it did decades ago. For social and financial reasons, many companies are forming new ways of thinking around the concept of work while expecting the same or greater output. Some companies have now gone to remote work, while other companies require a mixture of in-person and remote work. These ways of thinking need leaders and team members to seek new ways to learn and develop their skills.

It's ideal if we can make these ways of learning accessible for all who need it. People need more nimble and flexible ways to access learning while being able to achieve a good work/life balance. So while traditional classroom learning is good in some situations, it can be greatly supplemented with other forms of development that can better prepare leaders and team members for this ever-changing work environment.

We need to be willing to continually work on our skills, not just strategic techniques. We should be open to developing and nurturing relationships with team members, improving communication, casting and fulfilling a vision, handling internal injustices and inequities, taking responsibility, using critical thinking to solve problems, learning ethically sound ways of working with others, and leading with integrity. When learning these skills, we can get a clearer glimpse of our strengths and weaknesses and set goals around improvement.

Mentorship

When considering areas in which to develop leadership skills, don't overlook mentorship or life coaching. Whether leaders are interested in traditional classroom learning or digital learning, they can still benefit from establishing a relationship with a mentor or a coach.

Mentors can add value to leaders who are pursuing a more personal way to develop their skills. They also bring wisdom and life experiences to the relationship.

Because mentors or coaches can offer a one-on-one relationship, they can get to know those they're helping more personally. They can more easily see where their mentees need to improve or affirm them in areas where they are strong and thriving. And mentees can learn from this relationship and use these interpersonal skills to form a better collaborative engagement with those they lead.

If you're a leader who is mentoring or who is being mentored, be forewarned that there is an expectation of confidentiality. Both mentors and mentees make themselves vulnerable as they share life experiences and past successes and failures. Mentors and mentees must come to a place of trust if the relationship is to succeed.

If you're a mentee and don't feel comfortable with your mentor, or you don't believe you're able to develop a healthy level of confidentiality and trust, it's time to find another mentor. Every mentor is not the same. You will find that they may use different ways of connecting and engaging with you, and you may need to spend time learning which mentor style is best for you. Talk with trusted colleagues and others who might be able to make solid recommendations.

Although studies show that mentors benefit just as much as their mentees, the focus of the relationship should be the mentee. Be aware of mentors who spend too much time talking about their personal problems. That might be a sign it's time to move on.

Coaches and mentors can become lifelong friends with their mentees, but their main objective is to challenge them to meet their goals and overcome their weaknesses. They can also be effective at helping mentees explore and discover their potential. Though many mentorships are centered around organizational goals and education, I believe that good mentorships can positively affect other areas of mentees' lives. They may begin to see positive effects at home, too.

For mentorships to work, mentors and mentees have to be accountable to each other and make the time to meet. And both should make honesty and trust the bedrock of the mentorship, which will make their time together more effective. Organizations can benefit not only from quality mentorships, but they will see financial benefits as well. It's difficult to put a price on the development of current and potential leaders, but it will be well worth it.

Becoming a Learning Leader

We're leaders. We're busy people. But I want to encourage you to make time to keep learning. If you don't, you might not be busy for long! If you're interested in a growth mindset, here are some tips to make the world your classroom:[6]

- **Read.** In this digital age, there's no excuse not to find information that can help you. You may already have favorite writers, bloggers, or social media influencers, but be open to those you might not be familiar with. As you read, however, use discernment to discover what is true and what is false. The downside to the internet is that pretty much anyone can post anything, and not all of it will be true or helpful. Glean what you can, keep what is important, and discard the rest.

- **Share with other leaders.** Sometimes we find ourselves competing with other people or "protecting our turf" by not giving away trade secrets. But don't let competition keep you from learning from other people. Be willing to learn, but also be willing to teach and share from your journey. You don't have to follow all the advice you're given, but don't miss valuable lessons from those who have similar experiences.

- **Leave your organization.** When we've been in a place too long, we might hit a wall. We've climbed as far as we're going to climb, and we don't have anything else to learn there. But many of us stay because we're comfortable. We've started to do our jobs on autopilot, which means we don't even have to think about what we're doing anymore. This is the perfect atmosphere in which to become stagnant.

I'm not telling you to quit your job without a plan just to try something new. When you have other people counting on you, it's not wise to jump out without a parachute. I'm simply encouraging you to consider leaving your comfort zone if you need to because something better may be waiting for you.

When my director chief recommended that I leave the fire department and go to the OEM, I wasn't entirely sure this was what I wanted to do. Even when he mapped out his vision for my career and was willing to work with me to make it happen, I still hesitated. Not only did I love working for the fire department and didn't want to leave, but I had a part-time job that ensured that I could take care of my family. By moving to the OEM, all of that would change.

Ultimately, I agreed to leave the fire department, and despite some bumps in the road, it's one of the best decisions I've made. I couldn't let fear keep me from learning new things in a new place. I had to embrace the change so I could turn the director chief's vision for me into reality.

We should work to create an environment that is friendly to different types of learning opportunities. Not only will we benefit from continuous learning and skill development, but our team members and the organization can benefit, too. Organizations shouldn't limit themselves to traditional learning. While it is one way that will benefit some current and potential leaders, it's by far not the only, or most effective, way to train and develop leaders.

There are many resources available for people who want to be challenged and see more growth in themselves and their organizations. We should keep our options open and consider distance learning, digital platforms, peer-to-peer training, and mentorships and coaching. For a company to be viable and remain so, leadership learning, development, and training are crucial resources for helping people grow and provide value to their organizations.

"Leadership and learning
are indispensable to each other."
President John F. Kennedy

Chapter Nine

Passion

Growing up, I was surrounded by people who spent their lives helping others and giving to those in need. As an adult, I respect the sacrifices they made not only for those they helped then but for those who would come after them. Their example gave me the drive to do the same and to develop a servant's heart. I want to give back in appreciation for what was given to me. That's the reason I joined the military and served my country, and it's the reason I went into public service.

These avenues gave me purpose, and along the way, I discovered my passion. It took time for me to know what direction I should take. I prayed and asked for direction. I wanted the Lord to give me discernment and insight. Once I found it, I knew what I needed to do.

Unfortunately, many people go through life without passion or purpose. They go from day to day believing that their lives lack meaning. They are unhappy and unfulfilled. I want to inspire the people I lead and others I engage with to spend time finding their passion. Ask yourself, *What drives me? What do I have a deep and abiding passion for? What can I do that would give my life meaning and purpose?* Then pray about the answers to those questions.

In my journey, I've had to stay alert to God's voice and how He has worked through other people to give me direction. If I had ignored those who saw my potential or failed to spend time discovering my passion, my life would look different today. Don't be afraid to try something new or reawaken dreams and goals you thought were long dead. God may be directing you in a way you never imagined. Stay open to His wonderful plans for you!

Passion, Purpose, Peace

I lead with vision, but if I didn't have passion for that vision, I wouldn't be able to get the buy-in of my team members. The passion I have for our shared goals recharges me on days when I've dealt with problems and disappointments. It gives me energy, keeps me excited about what we can do, motivates me to forge ahead, and safeguards against many of the distractions that might derail my vision.

When people lack passion, they usually don't have a clearly defined vision. And while they may talk about what they would like to achieve, they will rarely take the right action to move forward. But my passion is the energy that fuels my work. It soon becomes obvious to my team that I'm not going to be standing still or stuck in the way things have always been done. I'm open to innovation, and my passion will be the driving force that will move the department in imaginative and productive ways.

Also, passion leads me to the next level: purpose. Effective leaders want to be taken seriously. We don't want to give the impression that we're excited about something today, but tomorrow we will move on to something else. Purpose is the substance around which passion is built.

When you know your purpose, then you can take your interests, desires, and enthusiasm about a job or a calling and transform them into your life's work. Through your purpose, you let the world know that what you're doing is meaningful for the long term, and it will be part of your legacy.

Passion without purpose, though, is useless. It's like having a car full of gas but without an engine. The car won't go anywhere. Purpose helps to give us direction. Without it, passion can devolve into emotions or make us go in circles. Passion often needs to be tempered so that it doesn't burn brightly for a while and then burn out. We must find that balance so our passion doesn't outpace our purpose or that we don't try to fulfill our purpose if we don't have a passion for it.

Finally, you arrive at peace. Every day that I serve the Metro Nashville community, I live into a sense of satisfaction that I'm exactly where God wants me to be and where I need to be. I never wake up in the morning dreading going to work. I don't question what I'm doing or why. What I do every day is so deeply satisfying and life-giving, that I'm confident that I've followed my passion into my purpose, and now I feel nothing but peace.

Making a Difference

As great as it is to discover your passion and walk in your purpose, it's even more rewarding when you can inspire that in other people. Your passion can be contagious as other people discover what drives and excites you. There may be people on your team, in your family, or at your church who are rudderless. They're not sure what they should be doing. How can you help others find meaning and purpose?

You could start small and close to home. Perhaps you could volunteer as a tutor or a mentor. Maybe teaching is more your style. Or you could find organizations that need someone with your skills and expertise to counsel and advise people who want to know more about what you do.

If you lead a team, check in with team members regularly to see if they are still passionate about their work. Sometimes the people we lead may feel stuck where they are, and they don't see a path forward. You could inspire passion where there is none or reignite it where it has gone out.

But as important as it is to be passionate, be mindful of not allowing your passion to become too intense. Use discernment and seek a sense of balance. Don't be surprised if some people in your circle resist high-energy leadership. They may assume that your passion will create more work for them and that they won't be able to keep up.

Passion can erupt about one project or another, and we may be fired up about each one. Sometimes we're good at starting projects or whipping up excitement about a mission, but we're not so good at follow-up and seeing those projects through. Our passion gives us a short attention span, and we don't always finish what we start. We leave those tasks to our team members.

This is frustrating for them because these half-finished campaigns may feel disjointed and unorganized as we dash from one project or mission to another, letting our passions get the best of us. We may come across as easily distracted and not dependable, not seeing anything through from start to finish.

To make sure our passion is an asset to our organization and not a liability, we need to be constantly vigilant with how we use passion in our work. Finding that balance can be hard for us when we have an intensity around what excites us. But when we consider how others perceive us and how important that is to buy-in from them, then we must be willing to know when and how to temper our passion without allowing it to burn out.

Having passion as a leader is great, but inspiring it in others is even better. You can't assume that the people you lead are as enthusiastic as you are. Engage with them and see where they are. You'll have to take off your blinders and focus outward to gauge their level of passion. But keep in mind that your goal is to inspire sustainable passion, not temporary excitement over short-term projects. Think long-term, and invite your team members to give feedback that will ensure their buy-in.[1]

The Missing Piece

Imagine opening the box of a 500-piece puzzle. You shake the pieces out over the table, clearing a place to begin assembly. Perhaps you're one of those people who begin with the corner and border pieces, or maybe you like to pick random pieces from the pile and try your luck. Either way, you work for hours, maybe even days, meticulously putting the puzzle together. Occasionally, you check the picture on the front of the box to ensure you're getting it right. As the picture becomes clear, you know you're almost finished.

And then it happens.

You have one more piece to go, but you can't find it. You search the box and under the table, but the piece is nowhere to be found. By this time, you've assembled 499 pieces and done all that hard work. But no matter how clear the picture is or how beautiful it has become, the whole puzzle is somehow marred because of the missing piece.

Some leaders have all the right credentials, but they work for years sensing that something is missing in their career. They can't quite put their finger on it. They've gone to training sessions and read books, but they can't figure out what's wrong. All they know is that their trajectory has fallen flat, and nothing seems to be going according to plan.

These leaders can't find the missing piece. They know they're lacking positivity. They find it hard to remain focused and motivated. They've lost any excitement about their vision or the direction the organization is headed. Even when they've moved from one C-suite to another or from one directorship to another, they still feel unfulfilled and empty. Should they change careers, go back to school, or quit?

In this book, I want to encourage leaders to be committed and confident, to have integrity and cast vision, to learn to communicate effectively and consider servant leadership, to be responsible and stay open to learning, and to be courageous. All of these are great qualities, but without the passion to motivate leaders, these qualities are useless. They form an incomplete puzzle that may have been meticulously assembled only to lack the missing piece: passion.

It's sad to see people with great potential just going through the motions because they don't have the passion to bring the needed energy and excitement to what could be a promising career. Without passion, we lack the inspiration to keep innovating and imagining the future. When we lack passion, we lose the ability to attract new people into our organization, which becomes fossilized and out of touch.

Passion is an important piece of the puzzle. We may believe we can substitute other things for passion, but that's not sustainable. Passion is the piece that brings all the other pieces, our skills, together into a cohesive picture that matches our vision, clarifies our direction and purpose, and keeps us engaged and on task.

Leadership is tough. We must handle organizational expectations, the needs of those we lead, and our growth and learning. Burnout is a reality for many of us as we try to keep our eyes on the vision and achieve all our goals along the way. There are times when our education, connections, and position aren't enough.

But sometimes our lack of passion isn't just about what happens at the office. No matter how hard we try to maintain a healthy work/life balance, sometimes that's just not possible. If we're going through a divorce, grieving the death of a loved one, or worrying about finances, we will struggle to maintain a positive attitude every day and approach work with the same passion as we do when everything in our lives is going the way we want it to go.

It's then that we can leverage our passion for what we do and find our way through the burdens of leadership or life in general. It's our excitement and intensity for what we do that can often help us navigate those periods of adversity. If we can hold on to that passion, we will see everything come together and coalesce around it. We may have to dig a lot deeper to get to it, but this is when we need passion the most.

If you're having difficulty discovering or maintaining your passion for leadership, perhaps it's time to reach out to trusted people around you or a mentor or a coach. They may be able to help you to regain your passion or perhaps explore a new one. Maybe it's time for a new direction.

In either case, it's a good idea to seek help to find that missing piece, to reclaim your passion so that you can continue to lead and serve. Other people are counting on you to help spark their passion, and once you find your missing piece, you'll be in a better position to help others.

Becoming a Passionate Leader

I don't ask of my team what I don't demand of myself first. If I can't approach my work with passion, how can I expect anyone else to do so? If you want to inspire passion in yourself and others, consider these simple steps:[2/3]

- **Focus.** It's possible to be passionate about several things at once, but that will distract you from doing your best in any one area. Confirm what you're most passionate about, and then focus primarily on that.

I'm not advising that you abandon all other interests. Know how to tell the difference between passion and purpose and activities that might be fleeting interests or those best reserved for your leisure time. Your focus will also give your team shared goals and direction.

- **Be dedicated.** "Dedication can be a powerful source of motivation and productivity when channeled appropriately." Like focus, your dedication leaves no question in your mind or the minds of those you lead that you know what you're doing and where the team is headed. Your inconsistency will harm your team, and you will eventually lose their confidence.

- **Be eager.** Excitement is fine, but it can be passive. When you're eager, you're more than ready to act. Remain open to learning new things or using your talents in new ways. Take advantage of any opportunity to be productive, and engage team members to get on board. Passionate people understand that they can leverage these new opportunities to help their team grow.

- **Persevere.** Passion will give you the drive to keep going, no matter what. Passionate leaders "will not give up; in fact, it only makes them want to work harder."

- **Stay Positive.** This may sound like a no-brainer, but sometimes it's harder than we think. Some people seem to have a sunnier disposition, and they may not struggle with being optimistic. Others of us may have to be more intentional about injecting positivity into our leadership strategies. Start with how you think. Change your mindset from one of doom and gloom to one of hope. Then communicate with positivity. It's difficult to inspire passion in others for your vision if what you say to your team is consistently negative. Finally, change the trajectory of your team by taking action.

You can motivate other people to be the best version of themselves. Your passion can be a source of energy and excitement as you bring those you lead into full alignment with your organization's vision. You can combine all your other leadership skills with passion to form a complete picture that displays your purpose and direction and to make a difference in the lives of others no matter where you are.

But some of us lose our way. Either we haven't yet discovered our passion, or we have lost it somewhere along the way. There's no shame in that. Some of the best and most effective leaders have experienced burnout, discouragement, and exhaustion. Our loss of passion may not be exclusively about our careers. We aren't one-dimensional. We have other areas of our lives that affect performance at work. When we're grieving or preoccupied with a medical condition, we may lose our passion because we don't know how to juggle everything we have to deal with.

However, with help from other people and the right resources, we can get back on track and learn from those tough times. Sometimes the fire we had at first seems to have burned out. But if we rake the coals, we'll find embers that are just ready to spark. Our passion can be those embers that can reignite our leadership and let that fire and energy burn bright again.

"A person can succeed at almost anything
for which they have unlimited enthusiasm."
Charles M. Schwab

Courage

Many of us grew up reading comic books or watching TV shows that featured superheroes. We may have dreamed of donning a cape and flying or using our special powers to rescue people from the bad guys. But as the saying goes, "All heroes don't wear capes." There are courageous men and women all around us who minister to other people in big ways as well as small, unseen ways. They may go unnoticed, but they make a huge impact nonetheless.

One of my heroes is my father, Arthur Swann. He was born in 1910. He lived through two world wars and other conflicts, The Great Depression, racism, and segregation. He was a humble man with a third-grade education, yet he excelled far beyond what was expected of him. He earned the respect of everyone he knew.

Dad taught me many great life lessons, most of which I didn't fully understand or appreciate when I was growing up. Like most children, I wasn't mature enough to value those words of wisdom. But as an adult, I look back on Dad's experiences and all the things he instilled in me, and I am amazed by how courageous and wise he was. One of the most important things he taught me was to love, honor, and serve God. My life is strong and successful because it's established on the bedrock of my faith.

Today, I'm trying to leave a similar legacy for my children. They are my motivation to get up every morning and work hard. Like my father, I want my children to have better opportunities than I had and to teach them all the important lessons that will help them through life. I want their future to be brighter. I'm not a superhero, but I aspire to be a courageous husband, father, and leader for the next generation.

Courageous Leadership

Perhaps you believe that to be courageous you must be fearless, but that's not realistic. Real courage is shown despite fear. Courage shines best during those times when you are the most uncomfortable or trying to navigate the unknown. The most successful leaders embrace the discomfort, the uncertainty, and the fear. They understand that these are all part of the difficulties of leadership.

To overcome my fears, I lean on God. Ultimately, He controls my circumstances, and He empowers me through His Spirit. As Paul said, "I can do all things through Christ that strengthens me" (Philippians 4:13). God's divine strength helps me to follow my vision, no matter where it leads. Verses like this one build my confidence in what God can do in and through me to help other people. I'm mindful of being courageous because I know God is with me in every situation.

When the director chief first talked with me about becoming chief of the fire department, I could relate to how Abram must have felt. God told Abram to leave everything he knew and go to a place he didn't know. He didn't have a map or GPS. He had no idea what lay ahead, but he trusted God, and he went. That's courage. Abram could have stayed with his family and all the things that were familiar and comfortable, but he had the faith to follow God's direction.

How many of us hear God calling us to do seemingly impossible things, but we shrink in fear? I don't want to let fear win, so even when I'm not sure what lies ahead, I put my faith and trust in God. Then I put one foot in front of the other, confident that I will arrive at the place that God will show me. When I trusted my director chief and his vision for my future, I took a chance that eventually led me to this position. But I had to rely on the strength God gave me to courageously move forward.

We struggle with fear because we allow our emotions to overtake us. To be courageous leaders, we don't have to pretend to be brave or fake our boldness. Eventually, people will see through us and know that we're not being authentic and transparent. So, first, we should lead with facts, not emotions. Our emotions are unreliable at best, and they lead us to say things at the height of our anger, grief, sadness, or frustration that hurt other people. Or we might take actions that we haven't thought through.

Second, we need to change our focus because our perspective—good or bad—often determines the outcome. When we put our emotions aside, we can then focus on what the desired outcomes should be for our family or our team. Changing our focus and our mindset will help us to move past the fear and concentrate on the needs of those we lead.[1]

Walking Through Adversity

Stressors are part of the peaks and valleys of our lives. It's not a question of if we'll encounter adversity but when. Unpleasant as that is, it's a fact for all of us. But we shouldn't let that be a setback. Where we can shine and succeed is how we walk through those times. How strong are we when bad things happen? Can we persevere and get on the other side of adversity? How do we handle grief, disappointment, and fear? What can we learn that will help us to be better leaders?

Whether we're dealing with stressors at work, grief at home and with family, or our fears for what's next, we can draw on available resources. There's no shame in asking for help. Even high-level leaders need support, and there are people in our circle who are willing to help us. But it takes courage to surrender control and seek the help we need.

We may find it difficult to be vulnerable because we are so used to controlling every aspect of our lives and our organizations, and we may feel as if getting help makes us appear weak. How can we be good leaders if we are weak? But if getting help will eventually make us strong, then it's worth it. Sometimes being vulnerable is more courageous than when we pretend nothing is wrong because we're afraid of what other people might say about us.

There are many situations when we need to demonstrate courage. We have to walk the walk when it comes to inequities and injustices that we encounter under our leadership. If we don't, we can risk becoming hypocritical. When we've worked to develop an environment where everyone can feel safe and valued, we must also deal with those persons who would derail that and bring about division and animosity. Those we lead are looking to us to deal with this type of adversity. When we don't, we break the trust we've built.

Are we brave enough to speak out against divisive team members? Are we willing to make tough but fair decisions? Part of being courageous is to risk being unpopular and to speak up for what is right. We may be tempted to hide in our office behind strongly worded emails. But our team members need to see us out front, standing up for them and bringing peace and calm in the face of injustice.

When we make mistakes, can we own them? Some leaders will do whatever they have to do to keep their reputation intact. Often, that means passing blame to others and being afraid to admit when they've messed up. However, great leaders understand how important it is to admit failure and mistakes. More importantly, they know how to use those adverse situations to their advantage. After admitting their mistakes, they turn them into learning opportunities that will help them later.

We also earn the trust and respect of our team members because they're looking for us to be authentic, not perfect. We may not give them credit, but they know that we're human and that we have the same capacity to make mistakes as they do. What they want is for us to be honest, real, genuine, and transparent. And when we take responsibility for our mistakes, they can appreciate that we're not afraid to be vulnerable, to be human. That's how we can model courage.

I want to inspire you to use wisdom before making rash decisions around adversity, but I must warn you that sometimes courage looks like saying and doing what other people won't. Sometimes walking through adversity looks like being passed over for promotion or recognition because you stood your ground and stuck to what you believed to be right. It's not easy being courageous. If you find yourself in a similar situation, this would be a good time to talk with your mentor or coach. He or she may be able to relate experiences that can help.

I look to God for help and courage. My faith is secure in the almighty God, and I know that He is with me, no matter what I face. I'm encouraged by what David wrote in Psalm 23:4: "Even though I walk through the darkest valley, I fear no evil, for you are with me."

That verse brings me great comfort. It's obvious why this verse is read at many funerals. When we experience great sorrow and loss, when adversity is all around us, we may be walking through the darkest of valleys, but we don't have to stay there. We can get through it and to the other side.

Heroes Yesterday and Today

The Bible mentions those men and women who exhibited great courage in obeying the will of God or those who stood firm in the face of adversity, danger, and even death. Abraham, Sarah, Joseph, Moses, Esther, Ruth, David, Solomon, Isaiah, Jeremiah, Peter, and Paul come to mind. The writer of the Book of Hebrews even does a roll call of the "Christian Hall of Fame" (Hebrews 11). He also mentions Abel, Noah, and Rahab. These are the believers who have gone before us, leaving us an example of courage and faith.

When I read about the biblical heroes, I find strength and encouragement, especially when it seems I'm facing impossible circumstances. I think of how God was with these men and women in their impossible circumstances. But the Gospel writer Luke said, "With God nothing shall be impossible" (Luke 1:37). When my faith has been shaken, I stand on God's promises and pray for the same courage that these men and women demonstrated.

God has given us contemporary examples of courage who are known around the world: Sojourner Truth, Helen Keller, Clara Barton, Nelson Mandela, Mother Teresa, Martin Luther King Jr., Ruby Bridges, Rosa Parks, Chesley Sullenberger. Although I look to these men and women as examples of courage, I also notice men like my father, whose name may never be known outside of his family and his community; but he demonstrated just as much courage to me as any person who has received global recognition.

Just as my father was a good example of courage for me, I invite you to look around and find those people who model courage for you. Those courageous persons don't have to be well-known or giants in their fields. God doesn't promise that we'll be famous or have our names carved on monuments, written in history books, or stamped on prestigious awards. Instead, He calls us to serve Him and those persons around us. Let us strive to live and lead courageously!

Becoming a Courageous Leader

The responsibility of leadership may be overwhelming. We may become frustrated because it seems we're not developing courage as part of our skill set. For some of us, courage may be an innate quality that we don't have to work hard to obtain. Other leaders will have to be patient as they build their courage over time.

As you grow in this area, you may face resistance from those you lead, or you might experience failures along the way. Don't allow fear to overwhelm you. You can be a courageous leader, and I want to encourage you on your journey. These are some of the steps I've taken to become a more courageous leader:[2]

- **Lead through action.** Don't let fear paralyze you to the point where you can't move forward. Leadership requires that you take action. Your team won't appreciate you if you pass all the work on to them. Instead, they want to see "that you are in the trenches with them." They want to know that you're pulling your weight in helping the team achieve its goals, too. I take an active role in leading my team. I never want them to think that I'm too passive or too afraid to do what needs to be done. I want them to be confident that we're in it together and that I'm walking right alongside them in our shared work.

- **Be decisive.** Courageous leaders have to "quickly make a decision and be willing to commit to that action." Often, we don't have the luxury of lots of time to research every aspect of what's before us, analyze possible outcomes, and conduct focus groups around what we think we should do. In many cases, we're confronted with situations that need our immediate responses, and we don't have time to waver. We can't afford to delegate or avoid it simply because we're afraid we might make a bad decision. We appear weak and ineffective to those we lead. We should own our decisions, even if we make mistakes, and take responsibility for them. Your confidence will inspire your family, your team, your congregation, or your community.

- **Be stoic.** As director chief of the fire department, I'm under a lot of pressure to get it right because many lives are at stake. When tragedy strikes, I can't let my emotions get the better of me. I have to stay calm and respond in a way that instills confidence in the public. Don't allow those you lead to see you panic in the face of a crisis. You might be afraid, but don't let your fear spread to others. Be an example of stability and bravery, even in the face of fear and uncertainty. Courage can be contagious, and your example can go a long way in calming an otherwise chaotic situation. After the storm has passed, the people around you will remember your response and be grateful for your balanced leadership.

Leadership isn't easy. We have to make tough decisions. Sometimes we succeed; sometimes we fail. We make mistakes. People have high expectations of us: to take bold action, to stand for what is right, to lead with integrity. They look to us to demonstrate courageous leadership, even as we're walking through adversity.

I encourage you to turn to your family, friends, mentors, and other trusted people in your circle for support. I also turn to God because the Bible is full of courageous people who serve as examples of overcoming fear, oppression, and adversity. And I look to contemporary heroes who bravely have fought against slavery, racism, discrimination, poverty, and other injustices. However, I'm just as encouraged by men and women who, like my father, aren't famous, but they have a strong faith and a belief in standing up for what is right.

These great examples of bravery confirm that we don't have to be rich or famous to be courageous. We don't have to be superheroes. We just must be willing to put aside our fear of the unknown, fear of others' opinions of us, and fear of failure. It may take time for us to build and strengthen our courage; but if we persevere, we can be successful, courageous leaders.

"I learned that courage was not the absence of fear, but the triumph over it. The brave man is not he who does not feel afraid, but he who conquers that fear."
Nelson Mandela

Notes

Chapter One

[1]"What Real Leadership Commitment Looks Like," Selene Crosby, Business Bank of Texas (April 14, 2014).

[2]"Building and Sustaining Commitment," Eric Wadud, University of Kansas Community Toolbox.

[3]"Great Leadership Requires Great Commitment," John Neufeld, ACHIEVE Centre for Leadership and Workplace Performance.

Chapter Two

[1]"Without Confidence, There Is No Leadership," Francisco Dao, *Inc.* Magazine (January 27, 2008).

[2]"12 Ways to Develop Leadership Confidence," Dan McCarthy, Pragmatic Institute (November 4, 2015).

Chapter Three

[1]*Uncommon: Finding Your Path to Significance*, by Tony Dungy with Nathan Whitaker (Tynedale Momentum, 2009); page 27.

[2]*Shrinking the Integrity Gap: Between What Leaders Preach and Live*, Jeff and Terra Mattson (David C. Cook, 2020); Kindle Edition.

[3]*Shrinking the Integrity Gap.*

[4]"How to Preserve Your Integrity: Consistently Making the Right Choices," Mind Tools.

[5]"Great Leaders Have Integrity," Sigma Assessment Systems, Inc.

[6]"Great Leaders Have Integrity."

Chapter Four

[1]"How Your Perception Is Your Reality, According to Psychologists," Jessica Estrada, Well and Good (February 7, 2020).

[2]"Why Visionary Leadership Fails," Nufer Yasin Ateas, Murat Tarakci, Jeanine P. Porck, Daan van Knippenberg, and Patrick Groenen, *Harvard Business Review* (February 28, 2019).

[3]"Why Visionary Leadership Fails."

[4]"How to Build Your Leadership Vision," Tony Robbins, TonyRobbins.com.

Chapter Five

[1]"10 Communication Secrets of Great Leaders," Mike Myatt, *Forbes* Magazine (April 4, 2012).

Chapter Six

[1]"10 Principles of Servant Leadership," Indeed Editorial Team, Indeed (February 9. 2022).

[2]"All About Others: Servant Leadership in the Modern Workplace," Angie Spencer, Biz Library (April 16, 2020).

Chapter Seven

[1]"How to Be a Responsible Leader," Kent Business School (May 20, 2018).

Chapter Eight

[1]"Why All Great Leaders Need to Be Lifelong Learners," Gemma Leigh Roberts, LinkedIn (March 9, 2021).

[2]"Why All Great Leaders Need to Be Lifelong Learners."

[3]"5 Ways Great Leaders Keep Learning," Ben Brearley, *Thoughtful Leader* (February 2017).

[4]"Good Leaders Never Stop Learning," Gerard Seijts Ivey Business Journal (July/August 2013).

[5]"Good Leaders Never Stop Learning."

[6]"5 Ways Great Leaders Keep Learning."

Chapter Nine

[1]*The Ordinary Leader: 10 Key Insights for Building and Leading a Thriving Organization*, Randy Grieser (ACHIEVE Publishing, 2017); Kindle Edition.

[2]"5 Ways to Rekindle Your Passion for Leadership," Richard Trevino II, *Entrepreneur* Magazine (April 9, 2020).

[3]"Passionate Leadership," Rise Performance Group.

Chapter Ten

[1]"How to Lead With Courage," Spectra/bridge Solutions.

[2]"How to Lead With Courage."